Fairy Tale Baking

www.apple-press.com

ISBN: 978-1-84543-627-8
QTT.FAYB

Conceived, designed
and produced by:
Quintet Publishing
4th Floor, Sheridan House
114–116 Western Road
Hove BN3 1DD
United Kingdom

Project Editor: Clare Sayer
Photographers: Ian Garlick,
Simon Pask
Designer: Lucy Parissi
Set Designer: Lucia Rosenwald
Art Director: Michael Charles
Editorial Assistant: Ella Lines
Editorial Director: Alana Smythe
Publisher: Mark Searle

Printed in China by 1010 Printing
International Ltd.

Fairy Tale Baking

More than 50 enchanting cakes,
bakes and decorations

Ramla Khan

APPLE

Contents

Introduction

From a young age I had an imaginative and creative streak, which, combined with my passion for baking and cakes, resulted in me setting up my business, The Enchanting Cake Company, in 2013. With my love of enchanting cake designs, this book was the perfect opportunity for me to showcase that imagination and inspire others to try and bring their ideas to life.

Working mainly in the wedding cake industry, I don't often get the opportunity to create children's cakes so when I was asked to write this book, I jumped at the chance to showcase some of my other cake decorating skills and the inner child in me began swirling with ideas. As a young child I had an old, dusty copy of the Brothers Grimm fairy tales and this was the inspiration for many of the projects in the book. I re-read all my favourite stories and got lost in a world of magic, princesses and evil queens. I finally narrowed down my all-time favourites and chose 15 of the most popular fairy tales – I hope they are yours too.

When designing the projects, I had to stop myself from making them more and more elaborate – it's all too easy to get carried away with such enchanting stories. The main projects may look complex but, when broken down into steps, they are really easy to follow and even the most novice baker will be able to wow their guests with their creations. Once you have mastered the basic techniques, why not try creating your own unique designs by experimenting with colours and other details?

There is a wide range of projects within this book. I wanted to focus on all baking, not just cakes, so I have included tarts, cookies, chocolate truffles, churros and meringues to name a few.

The chapters are perfect for a children's fairy tale-themed party. Each chapter, or fairy tale, has four projects so you will be able to create a range of sweet treats that not only look amazing, but taste delicious too. You will also find that many of the projects are interchangeable – a lot of fairy tales have similar themes, so use your imagination to adapt the designs to fit other fairy tales. Make a cushion cake for Cinderella's glass slipper, modify the Snow White figure to make a mini Thumbelina, or create snowball cake pops – the possibilities are endless.

The smaller projects are great for children who want to get involved with the baking and decorating. Encourage them to use their creativity to put their own stamp on their creations. Don't be afraid to try new things, and just use the decorations as a guide, while your children use their imagination to bring their favourite fairy tales to life.

I hope you enjoy using this book as much as I enjoyed making it!

Ramla

Basic Techniques

IN THIS CHAPTER YOU WILL FIND ALL THE TECHNIQUES NEEDED FOR SUCCESSFUL BAKES.

TIPS ON BAKING

- Always make sure your ingredients are at room temperature before you use them. This will ensure they mix well and don't curdle. If you have forgotten to take the eggs or butter out of the fridge, you can soften the butter in a microwave on low heat for short 10-second bursts, but take care not to melt it. Place fridge-cold eggs in a bowl of warm water for 5–10 minutes.
- Make sure you measure ingredients accurately, using measuring cups and spoons or weighing scales. Measurements are given by volume and in both metric and imperial; follow just one system.
- Always preheat your oven and prepare your cake tins before you start baking.
- Bake your cakes on the middle shelf of your oven. If you are baking in more than one tin or tray, swap the tins or trays around halfway through the baking time to ensure an even bake.
- To bake even cupcakes, use an ice cream scoop to fill the cupcake cases – this will ensure they each have the same volume of batter.
- When a cake is done, it will spring back if touched lightly. Also, a skewer inserted into the middle should come out clean with just a few crumbs. If it comes out wet, it needs more time.
- Oven temperatures may need to be adjusted depending on your oven – you may need to invest in an oven thermometer if the temperature gauge is inaccurate. Fan-assisted ovens should be lowered by a few degrees but refer to your oven manufacturer's guide.
- Make sure the cake or cupcakes are completely cool before you begin decorating with buttercream or other butter-based icing, otherwise it will start to melt and become a runny mess.

LINING CAKE TINS

For the best results and to remove the baked cake cleanly from the tin, use baking parchment to line your cake tins. Alternatively, you can use cake release sprays or rub fat all over the surface of the tin.

Grease your tin. Cut a long strip of baking parchment about 5 cm (2 in) longer than the circumference of your tin and about 2.5 cm (1 in) taller than the depth of the tin. Fold up 2.5 cm (1 in) along the long edge and use a pair of scissors to make snips at small intervals along this folded part. Wrap this around the inner wall of the greased tin, with the cut edges resting along the base of the tin. Cut a piece of baking parchment the same size as the base of the tin and place this in the base to fully cover it.

FILLING A CAKE

Once the cake is baked and has cooled, it is ready to be filled. You can choose an array of icings and flavourings for this next step. And experiment with different combinations to create your own unique flavour. Once you have your icing ready, cover it with a damp paper towel to prevent it crusting while you get the cake ready.

If you have baked the cake in one tin it will need to be split before it can be filled. If you have baked the cake layers separately, then you just need to trim the tops to make them flat.

You can do this using a serrated kitchen knife or a cake leveller. The cake leveller will ensure your layers are perfectly straight and even.

Place the first layer on a cake board, securing it with a little buttercream or ganache. Then spread an even layer of icing on the cake using a palette knife, and place the next layer of cake on top of it. Repeat this with the remaining layers of cake and then gently push down to secure all the layers. Remove any excess icing from the sides.

CRUMB COATING A CAKE

Once the cake has been layered with the icing, you need to coat the outside in another layer of icing to seal it in and to stop any crumbs from sticking to the final cake covering.

Take some icing and, using a crank-handled palette knife, spread it all over the sides of the cake. Make sure every surface is covered and work into all the gaps.

Use the edge of the palette knife or a bench scraper to scrape around the sides of the cake to remove excess icing. Do the same for the top of the cake, ensuring it is as flat as possible.

Place the cake in the fridge for 30 minutes to allow it to crust and harden slightly.

Repeat this process to finish your cake with a thicker layer of icing. You can repeat this process and build up the layer of icing as much as you like until you are happy that the cake is fully covered. For the final layer, run the palette knife or bench scraper under a hot tap and scrape again lightly to smooth the layer.

ICING CUPCAKES

There are lots of ways to ice cupcakes, with a huge array of piping tips now available, from grass tips to ruffle effects, but the swirl remains the classic way to decorate a cupcake.

Take a piping bag and snip off the end of the bag just a little narrower than the size of the piping tip. Place the piping tip inside the bag and fill with your choice of icing.

Squeeze as much air as you can out of the bag and twist the end of the bag to push the icing all the way to the end.

Squeeze the bag as you pipe in a spiral motion, starting from one edge of the cupcake, going around the whole cupcake, and moving inward until you reach the middle. Finish by releasing pressure on the bag and lifting upward.

COVERING CAKES WITH FONDANT

You can leave a cake that has been iced with buttercream as it is or use it as an undercoat for another covering. Fondant is most often used to cover a cake, since it creates a good seal, keeping the cake fresh underneath. It is incredibly smooth, giving a flawless finish. See the table below to work out how much fondant you will need to cover your cake.

Covering a round or square cake

On a clean, dry surface knead the fondant until pliable. You may need to lightly dust the surface with cornflour if it starts to get sticky.

Using a non-stick rolling pin, roll out the fondant to an even thickness of 3 mm (⅛ in), making sure you have rolled out enough to cover the cake top and sides. Measure with a ruler if needed.

You may need to lightly brush the surface of the cake with water to make the surface a little sticky.

Lift up the fondant and place it on top of the cake. Secure the top by gently rubbing the surface – this will also ensure you get rid of any trapped air bubbles.

Next, secure the top edge of the cake by running your fingers along it gently, making sure it is secure all the way around.

Then open up any pleats that have formed and gently press the fondant into the cake, leaving a skirt of excess at the bottom.

Use a knife to trim the excess and store this in an airtight container for use on future cakes.

Smooth the sides of the cake using fondant smoothers; this will remove any imperfections and create a smooth base. If there are any creases, you can use your finger to gently rub them and the heat

COVERING CAKES WITH FONDANT

Round cake	Square cake	Ball cake	Fondant (rolled to 3 mm/⅛ in)
10 cm (4 in)	8 cm (3 in)	8 cm (3 in)	275 g (10 oz)
12.5 cm (5 in)	10 cm (4 in)	10 cm (4 in)	375 g (13 oz)
15 cm (6 in)	12.5 cm (5 in)	12.5 cm (5 in)	400 g (14 oz)
18 cm (7 in)	15 cm (6 in)	—	700 g (1½ lb)
20 cm (8 in)	18 cm (7 in)	15 cm (6 in)	850 g (1¾ lb)
23 cm (9 in)	20 cm (8 in)	—	950 g (2 lb)
25 cm (10 in)	23 cm (9 in)	—	1.2 kg (2½ lb)

from your hand should smooth them out. To create a sharp edge, use the two smoothers at a right angle and gently squeeze the fondant into the corner to create more definition.

TIP: For really sharp corners, use chocolate ganache for your final layer of icing, since it sets really firmly, giving a perfect base for sharp edges.

Covering a ball cake

To cover a ball cake, follow the steps as above for rolling out the fondant.

Cover the ball and smooth it down around the ball until it reaches the base of the ball.

Then use a knife to trim about 2.5 cm (1 in) of excess all the way around the ball.

Lift up the ball and push the extra fondant toward the middle of the uncovered base of the ball.

Squeeze the excess fondant together and trim with a knife. Use the heat from your hands to smooth away the seam.

Covering a cake board

To make your cakes look really professional, always use a covered cake board, which looks much neater. Use a board that is about 8 cm (3 in) bigger than the cake.

Roll out the fondant to a thickness of 3 mm (⅛ in). Spread a thin layer of piping gel all over the board. Place the fondant on the board and use a smoother to get rid of any air bubbles.

Use a knife to trim off the excess. Attach a ribbon around the board to complete the look.

FLOODING COOKIES WITH ROYAL ICING

Many of the cookies in this book use a technique called flooding, which involves creating an outline or 'wall' with royal icing and then filling the inside with a slightly thinner royal icing. This gives the cookie a smooth and level finish.

Fit a piping bag with a small round piping tip, fill with a small amount of royal icing, and pipe an outline around the edge of the cookies. If your

cookies have a cut-out shape in the centre you may need to pipe another outline for the inner edge.

Place the remaining royal icing in a small bowl, add a few drops of water at a time, and mix until you get a slightly thinner consistency. To check, drag your palette knife through some of the mixture and count how long it takes for the royal icing to smooth over and become flat. Ideally, it should be 10 seconds. If it takes less than 10 seconds, the icing is too runny and you need to add more icing sugar to thicken it. Once you have the right consistency, fill up a piping bag or a squeezy bottle and flood the cookies up to the outlines.

STACKING CAKES

When you stack one cake on top of another to create a tiered cake, you must have adequate support in each tier, otherwise the structure will collapse. You need to dowel all cakes, apart from the top tier. There are lots of dowel systems available, but the most common are either wooden or plastic dowels, in various lengths, or you could even use bubble tea straws.

For tiered cakes, the sizes of the cakes are usually 5 cm (2 in) apart and each cake needs to be resting on its own separate board.

Start with the largest cake and place a cake board the size of the next tier in the middle of the cake. Use a scribe or pin to gently etch a line around the cake board, indicating where the next tier should sit. Remove the board.

Insert a cake dowel within the etched line vertically through the cake until it reaches the cake board below. Mark with an edible pen where the dowel starts poking out of the cake to indicate its height and then remove the dowel. Line up a few dowels so that they are perfectly in line on one side and mark the height along the dowels. Cut all the dowels to the same size and then insert them into the cake in a circular pattern, around 5–8 cm (2–3 in) apart. For larger cakes you may need two or three rows of dowels.

Once the dowels are in place, use royal icing to spread a thin layer of 'glue' across the tops of the dowels and then place the next tier of cake on top of the bigger cake, lining it up with the etched line. Repeat this with the remaining tiers.

COLOURING FONDANT

You can buy fondant in an array of different colours but if you are using large amounts of fondant in several different colours, it is often better to colour your own using a few drops of concentrated liquid or paste colour.

Roll your white fondant into a ball and knead until it is soft and pliable.

Using a toothpick, smear small dots of paste colour onto your fondant ball and knead it in until you achieve a uniform colour. Some colours can be very strong so add tiny amounts to start with and build up until you get the colour you need.

If you want to colour a large amount of fondant, a good tip is to colour a small ball of fondant with a darker shade than you need and then knead this into a larger white fondant ball. This is much easier than trying to colour a large amount of fondant.

To create a marbled effect, knead together two colours but stop before they are mixed uniformly. Then, when you roll it out, you will have a marbled effect. This works really well with grey and white or brown and white, particularly if you want to create natural stone and marble effects.

Gum paste can be coloured in exactly the same way.

TRANSPORTING CAKES

With enough planning and preparation, your finished cake can travel safely to another destination and will arrive intact and just as perfect as when it left your kitchen.

Always transport cakes in a clean, dry cake box made of cardboard, since this will stop condensation forming on the cake, which may cause colours to run.

Pick a cake box the same size as the cake board so that it will fit snugly in the box without moving around.

You can use a non-slip mat under the box to stop it sliding as you are driving. The best place to put the box is in the boot of your car where it is flat. But make sure you have emptied the boot and it is nice and clean, since you don't want anything falling on top of the box.

Aim to keep the conditions in the car nice and cool – in warm weather you will need to put the air conditioning on to stop the cake melting. If the weather is really warm you may need to refrigerate the cake for 30–45 minutes before transporting to ensure the icing has set hard. And make sure it is kept out of direct sunlight, since heat and humidity can also cause the fondant to melt.

Basic Recipes

MOST OF THE PROJECTS IN THIS BOOK USE THE SAME BASIC RECIPES, FROM BAKED CAKES TO ICING.

SPONGE CAKE

This recipe is ideal for carving cakes and is strong enough to be covered by fondant. The following table shows the amounts needed for each size cake.

Preheat the oven to 160°C (325°F) and line two cake tins (see page 8) the size of your cake.

Alternatively, you can bake the batter in one tin and split the cake before filling – just increase the baking time by 15–20 minutes and reduce the oven temperature to 150°C (300°F). However, baking in two tins will give a lighter sponge.

Cream together the butter and sugar in the bowl of a stand mixer (or using an electric hand-held mixer) for a few minutes until pale and creamy.

Meanwhile, sift together the two flours in a separate bowl and set to one side.

Add eggs to the butter mixture one at a time, along with a spoonful of flour to prevent them curdling.

Once all the eggs are just mixed, fold in the remaining flour. At this stage you can add flavourings to the batter (see page 16).

Divide the mixture between the two tins, making

Round cake	Square cake	Unsalted butter	Sugar	Eggs	Self-raising flour	Plain flour	Baking times
10 cm (4 in)	8 cm (3 in)	85 g (3 oz)	85 g (3 oz)	2	85 g (3 oz)	25 g (1 oz)	20–25 minutes
12.5 cm (5 in)	10 cm (4 in)	120 g (4 oz)	120 g (4 oz)	2	120 g (4 oz)	35 g (1¼ oz)	25–30 minutes
15 cm (6 in)	12.5 cm (5 in)	175 g (6 oz)	175 g (6 oz)	3	175 g (6 oz)	50 g (1¾ oz)	30–35 minutes
18 cm (7 in)	15 cm (6 in)	225 g (8 oz)	225 g (8 oz)	4	225 g (8 oz)	75 g (2½ oz)	30–40 minutes
20 cm (8 in)	18 cm (7 in)	350 g (12 oz)	350 g (12 oz)	6	350 g (12 oz)	100 g (3½ oz)	40–45 minutes
23 cm (9 in)	20 cm (8 in)	450 g (1 lb)	450 g (1 lb)	8	450 g (1 lb)	150 g (5¼ oz)	45–50 minutes
25 cm (10 in)	23 cm (9 in)	525 g (1 lb 3 oz)	525 g (1 lb 3 oz)	9	525 g (1 lb 3 oz)	150 g (5¼ oz)	45–55 minutes

sure you distribute the batter evenly between the tins. Bake for the time indicated (don't forget to adjust the cooking time if you are baking in one tin). The cakes should look golden brown when done, and a skewer inserted into the centre should come out clean or with just a few crumbs attached.

Remove from the oven and allow to cool for 10 minutes in the tin before turning out and allowing to cool fully on a wire cooling rack.

Wrap your cake or cake layers in cling film and allow to rest overnight before assembling the next day. Resting allows the cake to settle, making it easier to carve. If you can't wait overnight, make sure it has fully cooled for at least 2–3 hours before assembling.

Flavouring the cake batter

Add flavour to your cakes by adding extracts or natural flavourings. The following amounts are suggested for a 15-cm (6-in) round cake.

- 1 teaspoon concentrated extracts such as vanilla or almond
- grated zest of 1 lemon or orange
- 1 tablespoon ground ginger
- 1 teaspoon ground cinnamon
- 1 teaspoon instant coffee granules dissolved in 2 tablespoons warm milk
- 150 g (5¼ oz) dried chopped fruits such as cherries, blueberries and raisins

CUPCAKES

For cupcakes, follow the recipe for the Sponge Cake but omit the plain flour. For 12 cupcakes you will need the same quantity of batter as for the 15-cm (6-in) round cake.

Preheat the oven to 170°C (340°F) and line a 12-hole cupcake tin with cupcake cases.

After mixing the cake batter, spoon into the cases, ideally using an ice cream scoop. This will ensure a batch of evenly sized cupcakes. The cases should be about two-thirds full.

Bake for approximately 20 minutes on the middle shelf of the oven until the top springs back when lightly touched.

Remove from oven and leave to cool for 10 minutes in the tin before transferring to a wire cooling rack to cool fully.

CHOCOLATE CAKE

This recipe is for a 20-cm (8-in) round cake, but it can be adapted to other sizes by using the conversion chart on page 18.

- 200 g (7 oz) unsalted butter
- 200 g (7 oz) dark chocolate
- 1 tsp instant coffee granules
- 175 g (6 oz) self-raising flour
- 30 g (1 oz) unsweetened cocoa powder
- 350 g (12 oz) sugar
- 3 eggs
- 80 ml (2½ fl oz) buttermilk (or milk with a few drops of lemon juice added)

Preheat the oven to 160°C (325°F) and line two 20-cm (8-in) cake tins with baking parchment.

Melt together the butter and chocolate in a heatproof bowl, either in short bursts in a microwave on a low setting or set over a pan of just simmering water (make sure the bottom of the bowl doesn't touch the water). Mix until just melted, taking care not to overheat.

Make the coffee by mixing the instant coffee with 100 ml (3½ fl oz) boiling water. Allow to cool.

While this is cooling, in a separate bowl, sift together the flour with the cocoa powder. Add the sugar.

Beat the eggs in a separate bowl and add the buttermilk or milk and lemon juice.

Once the chocolate mixture and coffee have cooled, add them both to the flour and mix well. Then add the eggs and beat for 1 minute.

Split the mixture evenly between the cake tins and bake for approximately 40 minutes, or until a skewer inserted into the centre comes out clean.

Chocolate cake will shrink slightly when removed from the oven so don't worry if the dome flattens.

Allow it to cool in the tins for about 10 minutes, and then remove and allow it to cool fully on a wire cooling rack.

You may need to trim the tops of the cakes to create a flat top and this can be done using a serrated kitchen knife or a cake leveller. Wait until the cake is fully cooled before trimming, since the texture will be crumbly when warm.

If you are not planning on using the cake straight away, then wrap it in cling film and keep it overnight for use the next day. This cake will keep for up to a week if stored in a cool, dry place in an airtight container.

Recipe conversion chart

To bake a smaller or larger chocolate cake, follow the recipe on page 17 using the following amounts of batter. If your conversion calls for 1½ eggs, use 2 medium eggs instead of large. For baking times refer to the chart on page 15.

15 cm (6 in)	½ quantity
18 cm (7 in)	¾ quantity
20 cm (8 in)	1 quantity
23 cm (9 in)	1¼ quantities
25 cm (10 in)	1½ quantities
28 cm (11 in)	2 quantities
30 cm (12 in)	2½ quantities

CHOCOLATE CUPCAKES

Use half the quantity of chocolate cake batter to make 12 cupcakes and bake as for plain cupcakes.

COOKIE DOUGH

This cookie dough is used in a number of recipes throughout the book. It will make anything from 15–25 cookies, depending on the size of your cutters. It can be made in advance and chilled in the fridge, tightly wrapped in cling film.

225 g (8 oz) unsalted butter
200 g (7 oz) sugar
450 g (1 lb) plain flour
½ tsp baking powder
¼ tsp salt
2 extra-large eggs
1 tsp vanilla extract

Line a baking sheet with baking parchment. Cream together the butter and sugar until light and fluffy.

Sift the flour, baking powder and salt together in a separate bowl and leave to one side.

Add the eggs, one at a time, to the butter and sugar mixture, mixing well before adding the next one. Add a tablespoon of the flour to prevent the mixture curdling. Add the vanilla and stir again.

Add the remaining flour and mix well, until the mixture sticks together and becomes one large ball of dough.

Chill the dough in the fridge for 15–30 minutes, then roll out onto a floured surface to a thickness of approximately 5 mm (¼ in).

Using a cookie cutter, cut out the cookie shapes and place on the lined baking sheet. Chill in the fridge for 30 minutes – this will ensure the cookies stay flat and don't spread during baking. Preheat the oven to 180°C (350°F).

Bake in the preheated oven for 7–8 minutes until they stop looking wet on the surface. They will still be soft at this stage but do not overbake, since they will continue to harden when removed from the oven. Leave to cool completely before decorating.

BUTTERCREAM

This is the simplest icing to prepare and perfect for anyone with a sweet tooth due to the sweetness of the icing sugar. It's also really easy to flavour with natural juices, flavourings and syrups. The following chart will show you how much buttercream to mix for the different sizes of cake.

In the bowl of an electric mixer, beat the butter on high speed until it is pale and creamy. This usually takes around 5 minutes.

Add about one quarter of the icing sugar and mix on low speed until just incorporated.

Add the remaining icing sugar and beat for another 3–4 minutes on low speed. Add any flavourings (see page 20) or colourings at this point and mix well.

You may need to add a couple of tablespoons of milk to make it a spreadable consistency.

Buttercream will keep for up to 2 weeks in the fridge or 2 months in the freezer.

TIP: When adding the icing sugar to the butter, wrap a tea towel around the mixer to enclose the bowl so that when you start mixing it doesn't create a big cloud of icing sugar.

BUTTERCREAM QUANTITIES

Round cake	Square cake	Unsalted butter	Icing sugar	Total quantity
10 cm (4 in)	8 cm (3 in)	100 g (3½ oz)	200 g (7 oz)	300 g (10½ oz)
12.5 cm (5 in)	10 cm (4 in)	125 g (4½ oz)	275 g (10 oz)	400 g (14 oz)
15 cm (6 in)	12.5 cm (5 in)	150 g (5¼ oz)	350 g (12 oz)	500 g (1 lb 2 oz)
18 cm (7 in)	15 cm (6 in)	225 g (8 oz)	425 g (15 oz)	650 g (1½ lb)
20 cm (8 in)	18 cm (7 in)	250 g (9 oz)	500 g (1 lb 2 oz)	750 g (1 lb 10 oz)
23 cm (9 in)	20 cm (8 in)	350 g (12 oz)	650 g (1½ lb)	1 kg (2¼ lb)
25 cm (10 in)	23 cm (9 in)	400 g (14 oz)	800 g (1¾ lb)	1.2 kg (2½ lb)

VANILLA ICING

This is a lovely icing that is great for those who want a perfect white-coloured icing. It holds up really well in high heat as it's butter free. It can be used in place of buttercream in any of the recipes in this book.

- 150 g (5¼ oz) white vegetable fat, such as Trex
- Few drops of butter flavouring (optional)
- 5 tbsp powdered whipped topping mix
- 1 tsp glycerine
- 1 tsp flavouring of your choice
- 500 g (1 lb 2 oz) icing sugar

Mix together the white vegetable fat, butter flavouring (if using), topping mix and glycerine until light and fluffy. Add your choice of flavouring.

Add the icing sugar slowly and then mix on high speed for approximately 1 minute, or until smooth and glossy.

This icing will keep in an airtight container for up to 2 weeks in the fridge and 3 months in the freezer.

TIP: For a more real butter taste, use half white vegetable fat and half butter.

Flavouring the icing

Try experimenting with different flavourings to create a unique tasting combination. Add the freshly grated zest of citrus fruits or a few drops of vanilla or almond extract. Also try infusing teabags in warm milk to add to buttercream. Syrups and extracts also work really well. Start off with a teaspoon and just add to taste until you are happy with the flavour.

GANACHE

Chocolate ganache makes a perfect base for covering cakes in fondant but it's still creamy enough to use as a filling too. Ganache is simple to make, since it only uses two ingredients: chocolate and cream. Dark chocolate ganache is made with 2 parts chocolate to 1 part cream, while white chocolate ganache uses 3 parts chocolate to 1 part cream (or 4:1 in very warm weather). Try infusing chocolate ganache with different flavourings to add another dimension.

Dark chocolate ganache

- 400 g (14 oz) dark chocolate, either broken into smaller pieces, or use chocolate chips
- 200 ml (7 fl oz) double or whipping cream

White chocolate ganache

- 600 g (1 lb 5 oz) white chocolate chips
- 200 ml (7 fl oz) double or whipping cream

Place the chocolate and cream in a heatproof bowl and microwave in 30-second bursts, allowing it to rest in between.

Once the chocolate has started to melt, start stirring slowly and continue to melt in 10-second bursts until the chocolate and cream are fully mixed together.

Make sure you don't overheat it or the ganache will split and start to become oily. If this happens, refrigerate until it has cooled down, then mix it until it comes together again.

Ganache will keep in an airtight container for up to 2 weeks in the fridge or 3 months in the freezer.

Bring the ganache to room temperature before using. It may need to be warmed in the microwave for 10–15 seconds but take care not to overheat it.

ROYAL ICING

Royal icing was traditionally used as a cake covering on wedding cakes. However, with the rise of fondant it is now almost exclusively used for piping details on cakes. It holds up really well and is super strong, so it can be used for attaching decorations to cakes. It also gives a perfectly smooth finish and can be used for piping really fine details.

4 tbsp (40 g) powdered egg white
¼ tsp cream of tartar
80 ml (2½ fl oz) lukewarm water
500 g (1 lb 2 oz) icing sugar
Food colouring paste (optional)

Mix the powdered egg white and cream of tartar by hand with the water in a clean bowl – it will be lumpy, but don't worry, it will become smooth.

Add the icing sugar and use an electric hand mixer to mix on a low speed for about 4 minutes.

Add the colouring (if using) at this stage and stir until completely incorporated.

Store in an airtight container until needed to stop it drying out and always keep the lid on the container when not in use.

EDIBLE GLUE

You can use royal icing to stick heavier decorations to cakes but you can also make a thinner edible glue that is clear so it dries invisible.

¼ tsp tylose (CMC) powder
1¾ tbsp (25 ml) cool boiled water

Place both ingredients in a small jar with a lid and shake well. The mixture will appear lumpy but don't worry about this at this stage.

Leave overnight – the following day the mixture will have turned into a smooth, thick glue.

Sleeping Beauty

At the christening of a king and queen's longed-for child, seven fairies were invited to be godmothers. One by one the fairies went up to the child's cradle and offered their gifts: beauty, wit, grace, dance, song and music. But before the seventh fairy could bestow her gift, the palace doors flew open and a wicked fairy arrived, furious that she had been left out of the celebrations. She approached the little princess and said, 'When the child is sixteen she will prick her finger on a spindle, and die!' The king and queen begged her to forgive them and take her words back but the fairy refused to do so. When the seventh fairy, who had not yet given her gift, saw the king and queen crying, she said, 'I cannot undo what the wicked fairy has done. But I certainly can make it different. Your child shall not die when she touches the spindle. But she will fall into a deep sleep for a hundred years.' Hearing this, the king forbade everyone from spinning and ordered all the spinning wheels in the land to be burned, so that the princess would never touch a spindle.

The princess grew up to be a kind and beautiful girl and everybody loved her. The years passed and on her sixteenth birthday she wandered through the rooms of the castle. She soon came to a room where an old woman was spinning. Having never seen a spindle before she was curious. 'What is this? May I try?' The old lady said, 'Of course, my pretty little child!' But the moment she touched the spindle, she fell to the floor in a deep slumber. The king and queen laid her on her bed and were heartbroken that they would never see their daughter awake again. The good fairies took pity on them and cast a spell over the whole kingdom so that when the princess woke up after a hundred years, she would not be alone in the palace. Everyone, including the guards and the servants and the animals, were now fast asleep and a forest of thorns grew up around the castle.

A hundred years passed. One day a prince came from a far-off land, determined to find the 'Sleeping Beauty'. He fought his way through the forest of thorns and entered the sleeping castle. Soon he found the sleeping princess and was struck by her radiant beauty. He fell to his knees and planted a kiss on her lips, so ending the wicked fairy's curse. The princess opened her eyes and on seeing the prince said, 'Are you my prince?' The prince and the princess fell in love with each other and shortly after a great royal wedding took place.

Sleeping Beauty in a Bed Cake

You'll need to make the bed frame first so that it has time to set before you assemble the cake.

BED FRAME
Florists' wire #18
200 g (7 oz) brown fondant
Small amount of royal icing (see page 21)
100-g (3½-oz) cake lace kit

CAKE
1 quantity of 15-cm (6-in) round cake batter (see page 15)
300 g (10½ oz) buttercream (see page 19)
200 g (7 oz) white fondant
Edible glue

SLEEPING BEAUTY
200 g (7 oz) white fondant
Flesh, yellow and purple food colouring pastes
Pink petal dust
Black edible pen
Rejuvenator spirit

MAKE THE BED FRAME

1 Make the bed frame by measuring and cutting the following lengths of florists' wire: four 15-cm (6-in) lengths, two 19-cm (7½-in) lengths and two 11-cm (4½-in) lengths.

2 Roll a ball of brown fondant into a long sausage, then insert one of the wires through the centre of the fondant sausage. Repeat for each of the wires – for the four 15-cm (6-in) wires, ensure they are fully covered in fondant, but for the remaining size wires leave about 5 mm (¼ in) of wire sticking out of both ends.

3 For the four 15-cm (6-in) fondant-covered wires, take a toothpick and indent two small holes about 3 mm (⅛ in) from one end of the fondant in a 12 o'clock and 3 o'clock position. Set to one side to dry.

4 Roll out all but 1 teaspoon of the remaining brown fondant to a thickness of 5 mm (¼ in) and use a woodgrain texture mat to emboss a woodgrain effect.

5 Cut two bed panels for the front and back of the cake from the woodgrained fondant. The front panel should be 10 x 10 cm (4 x 4 in), and the back panel should be 12.5 x 10 cm (5 x 4 in). Use a cutting wheel to cut a curved border for the top of the bed panels.

6 Use a cutting wheel and ruler to score vertical lines in the brown fondant to give the appearance of wood panels; you can also use small cutters to make cutouts in the panels if you wish. Allow these to set overnight until completely dry.

MAKE AND ASSEMBLE THE CAKE

1. Preheat the oven to 160°C (325°F) and line an 18-cm (7-in) square cake tin. Make up the cake batter and pour into the prepared tin. Bake for 20–25 minutes, then remove from the oven and leave to cool.

2. Trim the cake to a rectangle measuring 18 x 10 cm (7 x 4 in). Split the cake horizontally and fill with buttercream, to give you a cake 5 cm (2 in) high (see page 13). Crumb coat with buttercream (see page 9).

3. Roll out and cover with white fondant, smoothing out any creases using cake smoothers.

4. Roll out a medium-sized piece of white fondant and cut out two pieces each 18 cm (7 in) long using a garrett frill cutter. Use a pear-shaped tool to frill the edges, then attach to the cake along the longer sides using edible glue.

5. Roll out a long thin sausage from white fondant and attach above the frill layer.

ASSEMBLE THE BED

1. Attach the bed panels to the front and back of the cake using royal icing.

2. Assemble the bed posts: first attach the shorter top pole to two bed posts by inserting the wires into the holes that were created using the toothpick and securing with royal icing. Do this for both bed poles so that you just have the two longer poles remaining. Allow these to set for a couple of hours.

3. Then attach the longer poles to complete the bed frame, by attaching in between the two half-assembled posts; use a flat support, such as a box, on either side to keep it propped up while it sets. Allow to set for another couple of hours.

4. Attach the assembled bed frame to the corners of the bed panels using royal icing. Roll the reserved teaspoon of brown fondant into four small balls and attach to the top of each bed post with edible glue. Allow to set for a couple of hours.

5 For the lace curtains, mix a batch of cake lace by following the instructions on the package. Fill the cake lace silicone mat and allow to dry.

6 Remove from the mat and use a pair of kitchen scissors to cut strips of lace approximately 16 cm (6½ in) long. Attach to the top of the bed posts by looping around the post and securing with royal icing. If you do not have cake lace, you can do this with thin strips of fondant instead.

MAKE THE PILLOW, SLEEPING BEAUTY FIGURE AND BLANKET

1 To make the pillow, roll out approximately 40 g (1½ oz) of white fondant to a 1-cm (½-in) thickness, then use a knife or pizza cutter to cut a rectangle 6 x 4 cm (2½ x 1½ in). Using your fingers, gently pinch out the corners of the rectangle to elongate them. Then gently flatten the edges of the pillow all the way around. Use a dab of edible glue to attach this to the top of the mattress.

2 Now roll out 2 oz (60 g) of white fondant into three sausages to form Sleeping Beauty's body and legs (these do not need to be shaped accurately since they will be covered with a fondant blanket). Attach these to the bed just below the pillow.

3 Colour about 15 g (½ oz) of fondant flesh colour and roll into a ball to form her head. Pinch out some of the fondant and elongate to form the neck. Attach this to the centre of the pillow.

4 Use pink petal dust to dust some colour onto her cheeks and also dust onto the space that will form her eyelids. Then use a black edible pen to draw a line along her lower lash line to form a closed eyelid.

5 Use some pink petal dust mixed with a few drops of rejuvenator spirit to paint on her lips.

6 Colour a small amount of fondant yellow and use a sugar shaper gun fitted with a mesh disc to extrude her hair (or you can make her as on page 39, step 10). Attach it in clumps to her head, allowing it to tumble beside her. You can make her hair look curly by twisting the strands.

7 To make the blanket, colour about 70 g (2½ oz) of fondant purple and roll out. Cut a piece just larger than the width of the bed and just long enough to cover her body. Use a quilting tool to make diagonal lines across the blanket. Place this blanket across her body, securing with a touch of edible glue. Make the blanket look more natural by creating folds in the fondant.

Spindle Churros

The secret to this recipe is the rich chocolate dipping sauce – pure indulgence.

MAKES 10–12

CHURROS
250 g (9 oz) plain flour
1 tsp baking powder
240 ml (8 fl oz) water
2 tbsp (30 g) sugar
Pinch of salt
3½ tbsp (50 g) unsalted butter, melted
2 eggs, beaten
Vegetable oil, for frying
10–12 wooden skewers

CINNAMON SUGAR
3 tbsp (50 g) sugar
2 tsp ground cinnamon

CHOCOLATE SAUCE
175 g (6 oz) dark chocolate, broken into pieces
100 ml (3½ fl oz) double cream
60 ml (2 fl oz) milk
60 ml (2 fl oz) golden syrup

1. Start by making the churros. In a large bowl, sift together the flour and baking powder.
2. Place the water, sugar and salt in a pan and bring to a boil. Add the melted butter.
3. Form a well in the middle of the flour and add the water mixture. Mix quickly until it forms a dough. Allow the mixture to cool slightly then add the eggs, one at a time, and beat quickly with a wooden spoon to form a sticky dough.
4. Pour the oil into a large, deep pan and heat to 180°C (350°F), or until a cube of bread dropped into it sizzles and turns golden within 45 seconds.
5. Place the dough in a piping bag fitted with a large star tip and pipe tubes of batter directly into the hot oil, cutting them off with kitchen scissors. Fry them for a few minutes until they turn golden brown.
6. Remove from the oil using a slotted spoon and drain on paper towels.
7. For the cinnamon sugar, mix together the sugar and cinnamon in a bowl, then toss the churros in the cinnamon sugar to coat. Insert a wooden skewer into one end of each churro for the 'spindle'.
8. Make the chocolate dipping sauce by melting all the ingredients together in a pan over a low heat, then pour into a serving bowl.

I cannot undo what the wicked fairy has done. But I certainly can make it different. Your child shall not die when she touches the spindle. But she will fall into a deep sleep for a hundred years.

Bramble Tartlets with Chocolate Thorns

Make the chocolate decorations in advance so they have time to set. You will need individual loose-bottomed tart tins.

MAKES 6–8

CHOCOLATE DECORATIONS
50 g (1¾ oz) dark chocolate, broken into small pieces

One day a prince came from a far-off land, determined to find the 'Sleeping Beauty'. He fought his way through the forest of thorns and entered the sleeping castle.

CHOCOLATE SHORTCRUST PASTRY

225 g (8 oz) plain flour
50 g (1¾ oz) icing sugar, plus extra for dusting
2 tbsp (30 g) cocoa powder
Pinch of salt
Pinch of ground cinnamon
150 g (5¼ oz) cold unsalted butter
1 extra-large egg
Splash of milk

CHOCOLATE FILLING

240 ml (8½ fl oz) double cream
50 g (1¾ oz) sugar
1¾ tbsp (25 g) unsalted butter
175 g (6 oz) dark chocolate, broken into pieces
Pinch of salt
100 g (3½ oz) blackberries

MAKE THE CHOCOLATE DECORATIONS

1 Line a baking sheet with baking parchment or a silicone mat.

2 Melt the chocolate in a heatproof bowl until it is a smooth consistency, either in short bursts in the microwave or set over a pan of just-simmering water. Remove from the heat as soon as it is melted.

3 Fill a disposable piping bag with the melted chocolate and snip off a small hole at the end of the bag.

4 Using the templates on page 186 as a guide, pipe leaf shapes onto the lined baking sheet. Ensure that the chocolate lines are touching each other so that they form a whole shape.

5 Pipe thorns by making curved triangular shapes and fill them with the chocolate. You can also pipe swirls and other freehand shapes. Place in the fridge to set completely.

MAKE THE PASTRY

1 Sift together the flour, icing sugar, cocoa powder, salt and cinnamon.

2 Cut the butter into small cubes, then cut it into the flour mixture until you get a sandy texture.

3 Beat the egg lightly and add it to this mixture, along with a splash of milk, and mix well until it forms a dough. Take care not to knead the dough or it may become elastic. Wrap the dough in cling film and refrigerate for 30 minutes to allow it to rest.

4 Remove the dough from the fridge and roll it out on a floured surface to a thickness of 5 mm (¼ in). Using a pizza cutter or knife, cut circles a little bit larger all around than your mini tart tins. Line the tins with the dough, then prick holes all over the pastry using a fork. Place in the fridge to chill for 1 hour. Preheat the oven to 180°C (350°F).

5 Line the chilled pastry cases with baking parchment and baking beans and bake for 15 minutes.

6 Remove the paper and beans and return to the oven for a further 5 minutes. Remove from the oven and leave to cool fully.

MAKE THE FILLING

1 Place the cream and sugar in a pan and slowly bring to a boil over low heat.

2 Remove from the heat and add the butter, chocolate and salt. Stir until completely melted.

3 Fill the baked pastry cases almost to the top and leave to cool completely.

4 Decorate with berries and the chocolate decorations and dust with icing sugar.

Meringue Kisses

Practise your piping skills with these delicate meringues to make perfect little kisses!

MAKES 25–30

240 g (8½ oz) caster sugar
3 extra-large egg whites (approximately 120 ml/4 fl oz)
Blue or pink food colouring paste (optional)

1. Preheat the oven to 180°C (350°F).
2. Line a baking sheet with baking parchment and pour the sugar onto it. Shake the tray so the sugar is evenly distributed. Bake for 4–5 minutes until the edges just start to melt. Remove from the oven and reduce the oven temperature to 100°C (212°F).
3. Whisk the egg whites in a bowl until they start foaming and then form stiff peaks. You can check this by turning the bowl upside down – the egg whites should stay in position.
4. Add the 'baked' sugar, a tablespoon at a time, while whisking on low speed.
5. Once all the sugar has been added, whisk on high speed until stiff peaks form once again. This should take a further 5 minutes. If you wish, you can add a few drops of food colouring paste at this stage, and whisk until evenly mixed.
6. Check the meringue mixture is ready by rubbing some of the mixture between your fingers – it should feel smooth, not grainy. If it still feels grainy, whisk for a few more minutes.
7. Once the mixture is ready, fit a piping bag with a large star-shaped tip and fill it with the meringue mixture.
8. Pipe onto another baking sheet lined with baking parchment, holding the bag vertically and squeezing meringue kisses that are 2.5 cm (1 in) wide, then release the pressure on the bag and drag upward.
9. Bake for approximately 30 minutes. You should be able to lift the kisses off the paper easily without them breaking. Leave to cool.

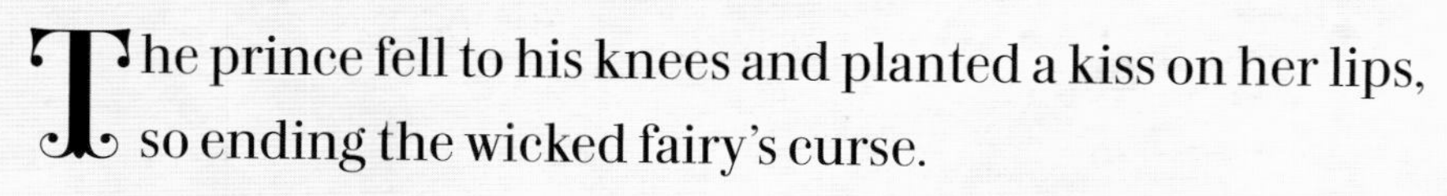

The prince fell to his knees and planted a kiss on her lips, so ending the wicked fairy's curse.

Cinderella

A beautiful young girl swept the floor in the kitchen of a great house and sighed. Her mother died long ago and her father remarried; a few years later her beloved father died, leaving her in the care of her wicked stepmother. She was banished to the kitchen by her stepmother and equally vile stepsisters, who never showed her the slightest drop of kindness, but instead treated her with contempt.

One day, amid much excitement, it was announced that the king was holding a ball to find a wife for his son, the prince. All the wealthy families in the land were invited, but Cinderella's stepmother would not let her go. Instead, she had to work harder than ever to sew new dresses for her stepsisters and help them prepare for the ball. They swept out of the house, leaving Cinderella all alone. Cinderella began to weep, when suddenly a beautiful fairy appeared before her. 'Do not cry, my dear,' she said, 'for I am your fairy godmother.' With a wave of her wand she transformed Cinderella's rags into a beautiful gown and her shoes became a pair of sparkling glass slippers. A pumpkin and some white mice became a beautiful gold coach drawn by four horses, ready to take her to the ball. Cinderella was overjoyed, but as she left her godmother warned her, 'Cinderella, you must be back by midnight as the magic will wear off!'

When Cinderella entered the palace, everybody was struck by her beauty, including the prince who danced with her all night. She was so happy she almost forgot her godmother's words. As the clock began to strike midnight, Cinderella ran down the steps, leaving one of her glass slippers behind. The prince declared that he would marry the girl whose foot fitted the slipper. The next day, the prince and his servants took the slipper to all the houses in the kingdom. When Cinderella's stepsisters tried the slipper they squeezed it on until their feet bled, to no avail. Finally, the prince insisted that the kitchen girl in rags should also try it on, much to the stepsisters' disgust. To his amazement and delight the slipper was a perfect fit. He had found his bride.

Fairy Tale Castle

For this project you will need one 15-cm (6-in) square cake and eight 5-cm (2-in) round mini cakes.

- 1 quantity of 20-cm (8-in) square cake batter (see page 15)
- 650 g (1½ lb) buttercream (see page 19)
- 1 kg (2¼ lb) grey fondant
- Cobblestone embossing mat
- 7–8 ice cream cones
- Edible glue (optional)
- 150 g (5¼ oz) pink fondant
- 50 g (1¾ oz) brown fondant
- 2 tbsp pale green royal icing (see page 21)
- Small pink sugar flower decorations

1 Preheat the oven to 160°C (325°F) and line the 15-cm (6-in) and the 5-cm (2-in) cake tins with baking parchment. Divide the cake batter between the tins and put the smaller cake tins in the fridge while you bake the larger cake for 30–40 minutes. Remove from the oven and then bake the smaller cakes for 20 minutes. Let all the cakes cool in the cake tins for 10 minutes before turning out onto a wire cooling rack.

2 Level the square cake layers and fill with some buttercream, then crumb coat all over (see page 9). Level and fill the mini cakes and then stack one on top of another (see page 13) to make the four towers. Crumb coat these four towers too.

3 Roll out the grey fondant to a thickness of 3 mm (⅛ in) and, using a cobblestone embossing mat, imprint the pattern onto the fondant. Measure the sides of the cake and use a pizza cutter or knife to cut four pieces to fit onto the sides of the cake. Attach these to the cake, taking care not to push too hard or you may rub out the pattern. Repeat the embossing technique and cut out a large square piece of fondant for the top of the cake. Attach this to the cake.

4 Measure the height and circumference of one of the towers, then cut out a piece of fondant to that size and emboss it. Place the fondant pattern-side down, then place the mini cake tower on its side and roll it across the fondant, attaching it as it rolls. Where the fondant meets, use your fingers to gently blend in the seam. Repeat for all four towers.

5 Make smaller towers for the top of the cake by using leftover cut-offs from the cake and mixing it with buttercream, as if you were making cake pops (see page 86). Roll the mixture into long cylinder shapes, wrap in cling film and place in the fridge for approximately 20 minutes. Cover these in fondant (see step 4).

6 Place an ice cream cone on top of each tower to check that they fit (you may need to cut them to size). Roll out the pink fondant and use a cutter of your choice to make tiles for the turrets. Attach them to the ice cream cones in a tiled pattern using some buttercream or edible glue. Attach the cones to the towers using buttercream.

7 Make the battlements by rolling out pink fondant to a thickness of 3 mm (⅛ in) and using a cutting wheel and square cutter to cut out the pattern. Allow this piece to dry for 24 hours before attaching it to the front of the cake. Use the same method to make sides for the cake in grey fondant.

8 Make a door for the castle by rolling out a piece of brown fondant over a woodgrain texture mat and cutting out a door shape. Attach two small balls of fondant for the door handles.

9 Make windows for the towers by rolling out a thick piece of brown fondant and cutting a window shape using a cutting wheel. You can use the woodgrain texture mat for this too. Attach the windows using royal icing or edible glue.

10 Spoon the pale green royal icing into a piping bag fitted with a small round tip and pipe vines across the castle and turrets. Pipe leaves along the vines using a leaf tip. Attach small pink blossoms to the vines to complete the look.

With a wave of her wand she transformed Cinderella's rags into a beautiful gown and her shoes became a pair of sparkling glass slippers.

Fairy Godmother's Wand Cookies

Use star cutters in different sizes to make these pretty wand cookies – and make your wishes come true!

MAKES 15–20

- 1 quantity of cookie dough (see page 18)
- 15–20 cake pop sticks
- Crushed boiled sweets
- 200 g (7 oz) pink royal icing (see page 21)
- Red edible glitter or coloured sugar (optional)

1. Preheat the oven to 180°C (350°F) and line a baking sheet with baking parchment.
2. Lightly dust your work surface with flour and roll out the cookie dough to a thickness of 5 mm (¼ in).
3. Use star-shaped cookie cutters to cut out large and small star shapes. Use the smaller cutter to cut the centre out of the larger stars.
4. Insert cake pop sticks into the shapes and place on the prepared baking sheet.
5. Place crushed boiled sweets into the centre of the larger cookies, then bake for 7–8 minutes. The sweets will melt and spread out to fill the centre of the cookies to resemble glass. Leave to cool.
6. Once fully cooled, pipe an outline around the edge of the cookies with pink royal icing. Add a few drops of water to the royal icing to make a slightly runnier icing and use this to flood the cookies (see page 12).
7. While the icing is still tacky, you can sprinkle it with edible glitter or coloured sugar, if you wish, to make sparkly wands.

A pumpkin and some white mice became a beautiful gold coach drawn by four horses, ready to take her to the ball.

Pumpkin Mini Cakes

You will need silicone half-sphere moulds to make these delightful pumpkin cakes.

MAKES 6

1 quantity of 15-cm (6-in) round cake batter (see page 15)
500 g (1 lb 2 oz) buttercream (see page 19)
450 g (1 lb) orange fondant
60 g (2 oz) green fondant
Edible glue
10 g (¼ oz) black fondant
2 tbsp royal icing (see page 21)
Edible gold paint
20 g (¾ oz) yellow fondant

1. Preheat the oven to 160°C (325°F). Make up the batter and use to fill 12 half-sphere moulds about two-thirds full. Use the back of a spoon to push the batter up to the sides of the moulds.

2. Bake for 20 minutes or until a skewer inserted into the centre comes out clean. Leave to cool for 10–15 minutes.

3. Slice off the tops of the cakes while they are still in the moulds. Use a small spoon to scoop out some cake from the middle of the balls. When the cakes have cooled, fill the holes with buttercream.

4. Spread buttercream on top of the cakes and flatten with a palette knife. Place in the fridge for 15 minutes.

5. Remove from the ball moulds and place the two halves together. Use a serrated knife to make a pumpkin shape by indenting six segments. Spread buttercream all over the cakes and place in the fridge for 10 minutes.

6. Roll out the orange fondant to a thickness of 3 mm (⅛ in) and cover the pumpkin cakes. Use your finger to highlight the indents and push the fondant into the creases. Use a piece of green fondant to create stalks and attach these to the top of the cakes with edible glue.

7. To turn a pumpkin into a coach, roll out black fondant to a thickness of 3 mm (⅛ in) and use the template on page 184 to cut a door. Attach to the pumpkin with edible glue. Fill a piping bag fitted with a small round tip with royal icing and pipe on the details. Leave to dry for 30 minutes and then paint with edible gold paint.

8. Roll out the yellow fondant and cut four circles, using the template on page 184 as a guide. Pipe wheel spokes using royal icing, leave to dry for 30 minutes, and then paint with gold paint. Leave to dry for 1 hour and attach to the pumpkin with royal icing.

Cinderella's Glass Slipper

This technique uses isomalt, which gets very hot, so make sure you wear silicone gloves. If you are working with young children it may be safer to use white fondant instead. You will also need a fondant shoe-making kit for this technique (see page 187 for suppliers).

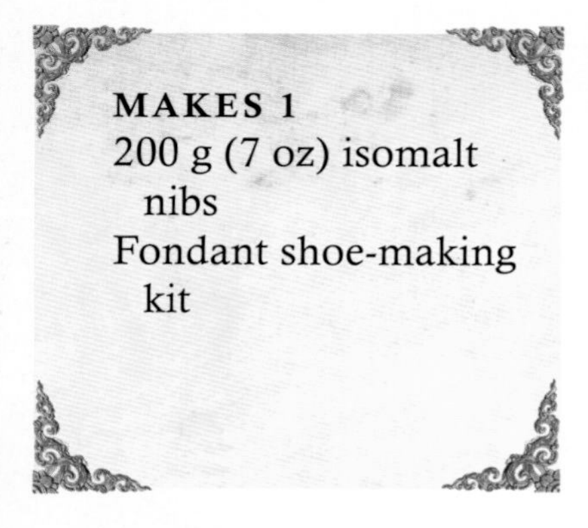

MAKES 1

200 g (7 oz) isomalt nibs

Fondant shoe-making kit

1. Melt 100 g (3½ oz) isomalt nibs in a heatproof bowl in the microwave in short 30-second bursts.
2. Once fully melted, pour into a heel mould and allow to set fully for at least 24 hours.
3. Melt 75 g (2½ oz) isomalt nibs as in step 1.
4. Place the shoe template from the kit under a silicone baking mat and pour the melted isomalt onto the mat, keeping to the template. If it runs over the template, allow to cool slightly and, while it is still pliable, trim the excess using a pizza cutter. Then place the whole mat onto the polystyrene shoe shape (with the set heel in position at the back of the shoe block) and secure it in position while it fully sets.
5. Once it has set, remove from the silicone mat and attach to the heel, either by melting the top of the heel slightly using a blowtorch or using some melted isomalt as glue.
6. Make the front of the shoe by melting another 25 g (1 oz) isomalt nibs and pouring this onto the silicone mat using the template for the front of the shoe.
7. Place the mat across a polystyrene half-sphere to shape it, and allow it to set before attaching to the front of the shoe.

As the clock began to strike midnight, Cinderella ran down the steps, leaving one of her glass slippers behind. The prince declared that he would marry the girl whose foot fitted the slipper.

Goldilocks and the Three Bears

There was once a young girl with hair so fair that everyone called her Goldilocks. One day she went for a walk in the woods. She quickly became tired and hungry, and pretty soon she came across a little cottage. She knocked on the door and, when no one answered, she went right in.

Inside she found a table laid with three bowls of porridge. Feeling evermore hungry, Goldilocks tasted the porridge from the first bowl. 'This porridge is too hot!' she exclaimed, so she tasted the second bowl. 'This porridge is too cold!' Finally, she tasted the third bowl. 'This porridge is just right,' and she ate it all up.

After she'd eaten the porridge she decided she was feeling a little tired. She walked into the living room where she saw three chairs. Goldilocks sat in the first chair. 'This chair is too big!' she exclaimed. So she sat in the second chair. 'This chair is too big, too!' she whined. So she tried the last and smallest chair. 'Ahhh, this chair is just right,' she sighed. But just as she sat down in the chair, it broke into pieces!

Goldilocks was very tired by this time, so she went upstairs to the bedroom. She lay down in the first bed, but it was too hard. Then she lay in the second bed, but it was too soft. Then she lay down in the third bed and it was just right. Goldilocks soon fell fast asleep.

As she was sleeping, the three bears came home. 'Someone's been eating my porridge,' growled Papa Bear. 'Someone's been eating my porridge,' said Mama Bear. 'Someone's been eating my porridge and they ate it all up!' cried Baby Bear. The three bears soon discovered that someone had been sitting in their chairs too, so they decided to look upstairs. Papa Bear and Mama Bear growled, 'Someone's been sleeping in my bed,' but Baby Bear cried out, 'Someone's been sleeping in my bed and she's still there!'

Just then, Goldilocks woke up and saw the three bears. She screamed, 'Help!' She jumped up, ran out of the room, out of the house and into the forest. And she never returned to the home of the three bears again.

Bear Cake

You will need two ball cake tins for this recipe, or you can bake round cakes and carve them into ball shapes.

- 1 quantity of 10-cm (4-in) round cake batter, baked in a 10-cm (4-in) ball tin (see page 15)
- 1 quantity of 15-cm (6-in) round cake batter, baked in a 15-cm (6-in) ball tin (see page 15)
- 1 cake dowel
- 1 x 15-cm (6-in) round cake
- 750 g (1 lb 10 oz) buttercream (see page 19)
- Brown and black food colouring pastes
- 100 g (3½ oz) light brown fondant

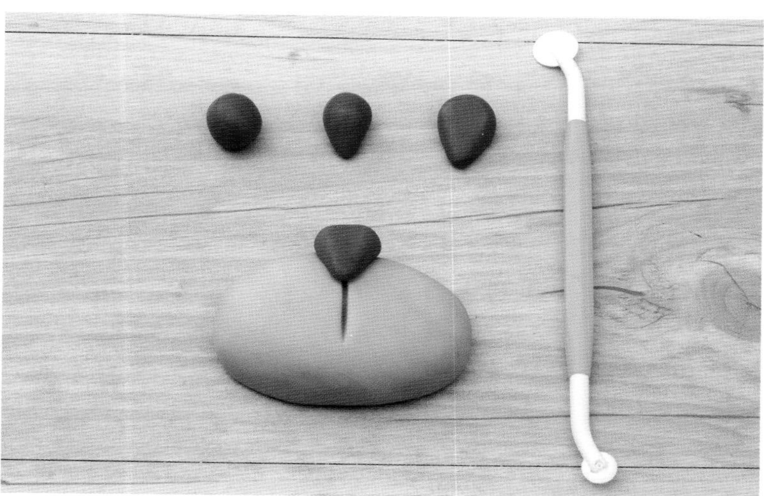

1 Split and fill the two ball cakes with buttercream (if you don't have ball tins, you can use round cakes and carve them).

2 Stack the 10-cm (4-in) ball cake on top of the 15-cm (6-in) ball cake and use a dowel through the centre of the body to secure it in position.

3 Blitz the round cake in a food processor, then add 115–225 g (4–8 oz) of buttercream to make a cake pop mixture (see page 86). The mixture should just stick together, but shouldn't be too wet.

4 Use this mixture to mould the bear's arms and legs and attach them to the body. Also mould two ears into semicircles and attach to the top of the head.

5 Crumb coat the whole bear with buttercream (see page 9).

6 Colour the remaining buttercream brown using food colouring paste and half-fill a piping bag fitted with a grass tip. Don't overfill the piping bag as the warmth of your hands can soften the buttercream.

7 Starting at the base of the cake, pipe the fur by squeezing the bag. When the fur is long enough – about 1 cm (½ in) – stop squeezing and pull the tip away. Repeat all over the cake, ensuring there are no gaps. Also pipe the strands in different directions to give a more natural fur look.

8 Roll half of the light brown fondant into a ball, then elongate and flatten it slightly to make a muzzle shape. Attach it to the head of the bear (you may need to secure it with a toothpick).

9 Colour 2 teaspoons (10 g) of the light brown fondant a slightly darker brown and roll it into a ball, then pinch the base to make a rounded triangle and flatten. Attach this to the top of the nose. Use a knife to make a vertical line below the nose.

10 Use the remaining light brown fondant for the paws and the ears. Roll out to a thickness of 3 mm (⅛ in) and cut circles slightly smaller than the paws. Use a small amount of brown buttercream to attach these to the end of the legs. Cut a small circle for the ears and cut in half, then attach the two pieces to the front of the ears.

11 Lastly, add black food colouring paste to the teaspoon of reserved fondant until you have a strong black colour. Roll the black fondant into two balls and attach them above the nose for the bear's eyes.

TIP

If you can't find ready-made dulce de leche, you can make it using a tin of sweetened condensed milk. Place the unopened tin in a pan of water and bring to a boil. Simmer for 4 hours, topping up the water in the pan if necessary, then remove the tin from the water and let it cool completely before opening.

Inside she found a table laid with three bowls of porridge. Feeling evermore hungry, Goldilocks tasted the porridge from the first bowl.

Caramel Porridge Flapjack

Goldilocks would be sure to gobble up these delicious flapjack treats!

MAKES 16 SQUARES

FLAPJACK

115 g (4 oz) unsalted butter
125 g (4½ oz) dark brown sugar
3 tbsp golden syrup
300 g (10½ oz) rolled oats

CARAMEL TOPPING

400-g (14-oz) tin of ready-made caramel or dulce de leche (see Tip, opposite)
200 g (7 oz) white chocolate, broken into pieces
150 g (5¼ oz) icing sugar

1. Line a 15-cm (6-in) square cake tin with baking parchment.
2. Melt together the butter, sugar and golden syrup in a pan over low heat. Tip the oats into the pan and stir to coat well.
3. Pour into the prepared cake tin and push down using the back of a spoon to spread the flapjack mixture evenly. Chill in the fridge while you prepare the caramel topping.
4. Melt together the caramel and white chocolate in a pan over low heat until smooth. Remove from the heat and thoroughly stir in the icing sugar.
5. Pour this over the flapjack in the cake tin and spread evenly using a palette knife.
6. Refrigerate for 2–3 hours until set, then remove from the cake tin and cut into squares.

So Goldilocks tried the last and smallest chair. 'Ahhh, this chair is just right,' she sighed. But just as she sat down it broke into pieces!

Chocolate Chair Cupcakes

Which chair has Goldilocks been sitting in? Make one or two broken chairs by leaving off one of the legs.

MAKES 4

- 300 g (10½ oz) dark chocolate chips, plus extra for glueing
- 20 g (¾ oz) fondant
- 6 large plastic straws, ideally 1 cm (½ in) in diameter
- 50 g (1¾ oz) light brown fondant
- 4 cupcakes (see page 16)
- 500 g (1 lb 2 oz) buttercream (see page 19)

MAKE THE CHAIRS

1. Melt the chocolate (see page 31) and stir until smooth.
2. Roll the fondant into six balls, and insert the straws into them so that they stay upright. Pour the melted chocolate into the straws, so that they fill all the way to the top. Place in the fridge overnight to set.
3. Pour the remaining melted chocolate into a 12.5-cm (5-in) square cake tin lined with baking parchment and chill overnight.
4. Carefully cut away the straw so you are left with long cylinders of chocolate for the chair legs and backs. Heat a knife under hot running water and slice the chocolate cylinders into four equal pieces, giving you a total of 24 pieces (six for each chair).
5. Remove the chocolate from the cake tin and use a hot knife to slice into four 5-cm (2-in) squares and four 2.5-cm (1 in) squares.
6. You will need a little melted chocolate to assemble the chairs. For the seat of each chair, attach four legs to each larger chocolate square. Place in the fridge to set.
7. For the back of each chair, attach two cylinder pieces to either side of the smaller squares using a little melted chocolate. Refrigerate to set.
8. Once the pieces have set, attach the chair backs to the chair seats using melted chocolate. Refrigerate to set.

ASSEMBLE THE CUPCAKES

1. Roll out the fondant to a thickness of 3 mm (⅛ in) and use a woodgrain texture mat to emboss it. Cut four circles the same diameter as the cupcakes and use a cutting wheel to make horizontal lines across the fondant. Allow to dry for 3 hours.
2. Pipe a swirl of buttercream on top of each cupcake and top with the embossed fondant circles. Place the chairs on top of the cupcakes to complete, using a little melted chocolate to secure.

Gingerbread Bed

Make your very own fairy tale bed out of gingerbread and fill with sweets!

GINGERBREAD

115 g (4 oz) unsalted butter
115 g (4 oz) dark brown sugar
2 tbsp golden syrup
1 tbsp black treacle
300 g (10½ oz) plain flour
1 tsp bicarbonate of soda
2 tsp ground ginger
½ tsp ground cinnamon

DECORATION

3 tbsp royal icing (see page 21)
Assortment of sweets

1. Preheat the oven to 200°C (400°F).
2. Make the gingerbread dough, following steps 2–3 of the Gingerbread House (see page 68).
3. Place the dough on a large sheet of baking parchment and roll it out to a thickness of approximately 1 cm (½ in).
4. Cut out five panels for the front, back, two sides and base of the bed. The front panel is 5 x 9 cm (2 x 3½ in), the back panel is 7.5 x 9 cm (3 x 3½ in), the two side panels are each 2.5 x 12.5 cm (1 x 5 in) and the base is 7.5 x 12.5 cm (3 x 5 in).
5. Use small heart-shaped cutters to cut hearts along the bed panels.
6. Place the cut pieces, still on the baking parchment, onto a baking sheet and bake for 10–12 minutes until the surface is no longer shiny and feels slightly firm. The gingerbread will harden once it is out of the oven so be careful not to overbake. Leave to cool.
7. Once the pieces are fully cool, you can assemble them using royal icing. Place the royal icing in a piping bag fitted with a round tip.
8. Place the bottom panel in position, pipe a line of royal icing along the sides, and attach the side panels. Place tin cans on either side to support them while they dry.
9. Attach the front and back panels in the same way and support them while they fully set.
10. Pipe a royal icing outline around the hearts and pipe swirls and dots to decorate the bed. Finish by filling the bed with an assortment of sweets.

Goldilocks was very tired by this time, so she went upstairs to the bedroom. She lay down in the first bed, but it was too hard.

Jack and the Beanstalk

In a land far away, there was a young boy called Jack who lived with his mother. They were very poor and one day Jack's mother told him to take their only cow to market, since they were desperate for money to buy food. 'Make sure you get a good price for her,' Jack's mother called as he set off.

Jack walked along the road and soon met an old man. 'Where are you going, young man?' asked the stranger. When Jack told him that he was going to sell the cow, the old man made him an offer. 'I will buy your cow from you in exchange for these magic beans,' he said, holding out his hand. Jack was not the cleverest of fellows so he took the beans and gave the man the cow. When he arrived home his mother was furious. 'You fool,' she said, 'now we will have nothing to eat!' With that she threw the beans out of the window and sent Jack to bed.

The next day, when Jack woke up in the morning and looked out of the window, he saw that a huge beanstalk had grown from his magic beans! It was so tall that he could not see the top. He started climbing and climbing and before long he had reached a kingdom in the sky. There lived a giant and his wife. Jack went inside the house and found the giant's wife in the kitchen. Jack said, 'Could you please give me something to eat? I am so hungry!' The kind wife gave him bread and some milk.

While he was eating, the giant came home. The giant was very big and looked very fearsome. Jack was terrified and went and hid inside. The giant cried, 'Fee-fi-fo-fum, I smell the blood of an Englishman. Be he alive, or be he dead, I'll grind his bones to make my bread!' The wife said, 'There is no boy in here!' From his hiding place, Jack watched the giant counting a huge pile of coins and playing on a golden harp. When he said to his hen, 'Lay!', Jack watched in amazement as the hen laid a golden egg. As soon as the giant fell asleep, Jack grabbed the hen and the harp and ran to the beanstalk. As he started climbing down, he heard the giant thundering after him. But Jack was too fast for him. As soon as he reached the ground he ran home to fetch his axe and began to chop the beanstalk. The giant fell and died. Jack and his mother were now very rich and they lived happily ever after.

Beanstalk Cake

Top this beanstalk cake with meringue clouds to show just how tall it is!

1 quantity of 20-cm (8-in) round cake batter (see page 15)
750 g (1 lb 10 oz) buttercream (see page 19)
1 long cake dowel or wooden skewer
1 kg (2¼ lb) fondant
Green food colouring paste
Edible glue
Green gum paste
Green and brown petal dusts
Meringue Clouds (see page 60)

1. Preheat the oven to 160°C (325°F). Line three 7.5-cm (3-in) cake tins with baking parchment.
2. Divide the cake batter equally between the three tins and bake for 20–30 minutes, until the cakes turn a light golden brown and a skewer inserted into the centre comes out clean.
3. Leave to cool, then, using a serrated knife, slice off the domed tops and split all three cakes in half horizontally.
4. Layer the cakes with buttercream so they form a tall tower (see page 13). You may need to insert a long dowel or wooden skewer through the middle for support.
5. Crumb coat the tower with buttercream (see page 9).
6. Colour the fondant green and roll it out to a thickness of approximately 5 mm (¼ in).
7. Measure the height and circumference of the tower cake. Cut a rectangle of green fondant to the same dimensions. Lay the tower on its side on top of the fondant and gently roll it along so that the cake picks up the fondant.
8. Where the two ends of the fondant meet, gently rub the seam together. Position the tower upright.
9. Roll out thick sausages of fondant and use edible glue to attach these to the base of the cake at varying heights, pushing the edges of the sausages into the cake to flatten and resemble growing roots.

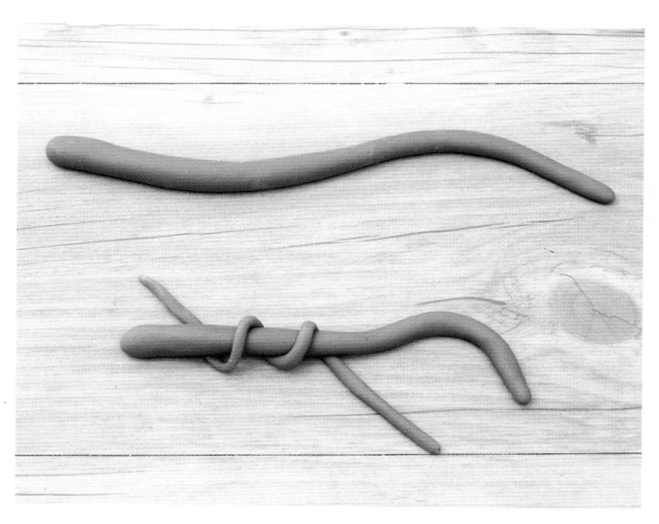

10 Split the sausages into two or three slices at the base of the cake and roll each one between your fingers to elongate and create the end of the roots.

11 Then roll out long sausages of fondant and wrap these around the cake, attaching them with edible glue. Make them different sizes to create a more natural look.

12 For some of these sausages, wind smaller strips of fondant around them to resemble growing vines.

13 Using a leaf cutter, cut leaves from thinly rolled-out green gum paste. Attach the leaves near the top of the vines.

14 Gather the vines at the top of the cake and smooth out to create a flat base.

15 Once all the fondant is fully dry, use a dark green petal dust to dust from the base of the cake to the middle to create an ombré effect. Then use brown petal dust to highlight the roots at the base of the beanstalk.

16 Complete the look by topping with Meringue Clouds (see page 60).

Meringue Clouds

These delicate clouds are made from piped meringue decorated with gold royal icing.

MAKES 8–12

240 g (8½ oz) caster sugar

3 large egg whites (approximately 120 ml/4 fl oz)

Small amount of royal icing (see page 21)

Edible gold paint

1 Preheat the oven to 180°C (350°F). Line a baking sheet with baking parchment and pour the sugar onto it in an even layer. Bake for 4–5 minutes until the edges just start to melt. Remove from the oven and reduce the temperature to 100°C (212°F).

2 Beat the egg whites until they start foaming and then form stiff peaks. Add the sugar, a spoon at a time, whisking on low speed.

3 Once all the sugar has been added, whisk on high speed until stiff peaks form once again. This should take a further 5 minutes. Check the meringue mixture is ready – it should feel smooth, not grainy. If it still feels grainy, whisk for a few more minutes.

4 Fit a piping bag with a star-shaped tip and fill it with the meringue mixture. Pipe onto the lined baking sheet, holding the bag vertically. Squeeze a blob, then release the pressure on the bag and make a counterclockwise movement to detach the meringue. Don't pull upward as the blob needs to stay round.

5 For each cloud, continue piping a few blobs next to each other, making sure they touch. Make the clouds different shapes and sizes to resemble real clouds.

6 Bake for approximately 30 minutes. You should be able to lift them off the baking parchment easily without them breaking. Leave to cool.

7 Once they are fully cool, fill a piping bag fitted with a leaf tip with royal icing and pipe the harp outline. Remove the leaf tip and fit a small round tip. Pipe vertical lines inside the outline to resemble strings.

8 Leave to fully dry, then carefully paint the harps with edible gold paint.

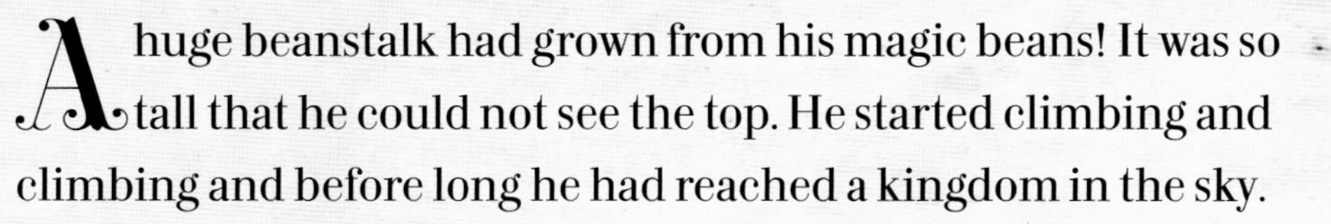

A huge beanstalk had grown from his magic beans! It was so tall that he could not see the top. He started climbing and climbing and before long he had reached a kingdom in the sky.

Chocolate Chip Cookies

Are those chocolate chips or 'magic beans' in your cookies?

MAKES 10–12

150 g (5¼ oz) butter, softened
100 g (3½ oz) light brown sugar
50 g (1¾ oz) sugar
1 extra-large egg
250 g (9 oz) plain flour
1 tsp baking powder
½ tsp bicarbonate of soda
Pinch of salt
200 g (7 oz) milk chocolate chips

1. Preheat the oven to 180°C (350°F). Line a baking sheet with baking parchment.
2. Put the butter and sugars into a bowl and beat until creamy.
3. Add the egg, along with a tablespoon of flour, and mix well.
4. Sift the flour, baking powder, bicarbonate of soda and salt into a bowl, then add to the butter mixture, mixing well. Fold in the chocolate chips.
5. Use a tablespoon to place spoonfuls of the mixture on the baking sheet, leaving enough space in between to allow for the cookies to spread.
6. Bake for 8–10 minutes until the cookies turn a light golden brown but still feel slightly soft.
7. Remove from the oven and leave to cool slightly, then transfer to a wire cooling rack to cool fully.

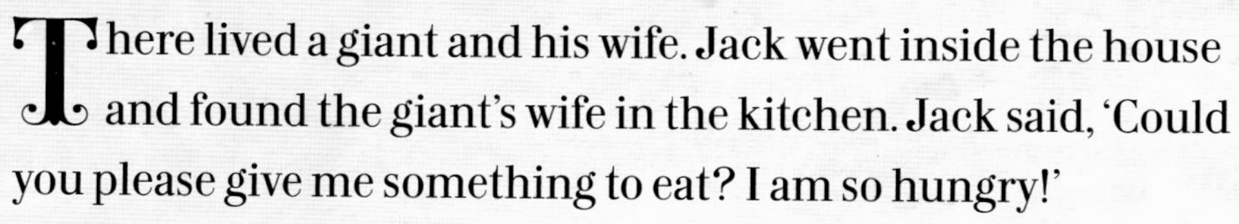

There lived a giant and his wife. Jack went inside the house and found the giant's wife in the kitchen. Jack said, 'Could you please give me something to eat? I am so hungry!'

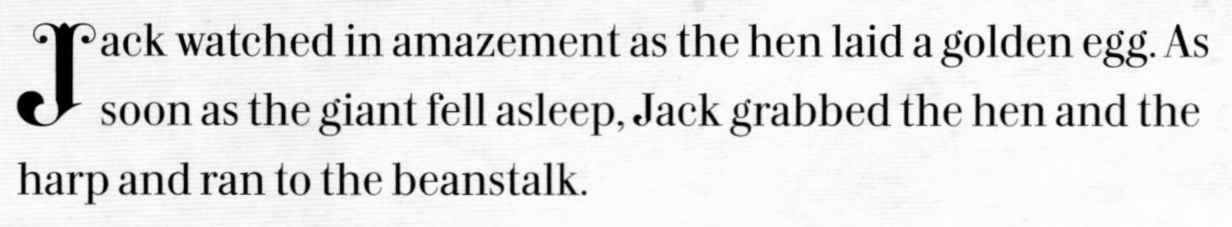

Jack watched in amazement as the hen laid a golden egg. As soon as the giant fell asleep, Jack grabbed the hen and the harp and ran to the beanstalk.

Golden Eggs

You will need silicone egg moulds to make these.

MAKES 15–18

200 g (7 oz) dark, milk or white chocolate, broken into pieces

Edible gold leaf or flakes – or gold lustre dust and rejuvenator spirit

1. Melt the chocolate in a bowl over a pan of simmering water. Alternatively, melt in a microwave in 30-second intervals.
2. Pour the melted chocolate into the egg moulds and fill to the top. Level off with a spatula or palette knife, then place in the fridge to set for a couple of hours.
3. Once fully set, remove the halves from the mould. Stick them together using a little melted chocolate and return to the fridge to set.
4. Once set, cover the eggs in gold leaf. Make sure you use gold leaf that comes on a backing sheet, not loose leaf, since this will give you more control over placement. Place the gold leaf on the eggs and gently rub the backing sheet with your finger to attach to the chocolate.
5. Once you have attached it, use a paintbrush to brush gently over the eggs to remove any loose bits of gold leaf.
6. If there are any gaps where the gold leaf has not attached, use a little warm water to dampen the eggs slightly in the gap and then repeat the gold leaf application.
7. Alternatively, you can also use gold-leaf flakes to sprinkle over the top of the eggs, or if gold leaf is unavailable, use gold lustre dust mixed with a little rejuvenator spirit to make a paste and paint this on.

Hansel and Gretel

At the edge of a forest, there lived a woodcutter with his two children and their stepmother. This was a time of great hardship and there was very little to eat, so the wicked stepmother came up with a plan. She persuaded her husband to take the children deep into the forest and leave them there to starve. But Hansel overheard their plan and crept out of the house to gather pockets full of white pebbles, telling his sister that he would not let her starve.

The following morning the family headed deep into the woods and when the children fell asleep they abandoned them there. But thanks to Hansel's cunning plan they followed the trail of white pebbles home, much to their stepmother's horror. The next day they set off into the forest again. This time Hansel left a trail of breadcrumbs. However, when the children found themselves deserted again, they were dismayed to find that the trail of breadcrumbs had been eaten by birds. They wandered deeper into the forest, feeling increasingly desperate.

Suddenly, the children entered a clearing where the most marvellous sight met their eyes – a little house made entirely of gingerbread, with windows of clear sugar and the walls and roof covered in cakes and candy canes. Starving, they fell upon the house and started to eat. An old woman appeared and invited them in with the promise of a place to sleep. Unaware that the woman was actually a wicked witch, the children entered the cottage.

As soon as the children were inside, the witch forced Gretel to become her slave and locked Hansel in a cage. The witch fed Hansel well and as the days became weeks the children realised that she was fattening him up to eat him. Every few days the witch, who was nearly blind, would pinch his finger to see if he was fat enough, but the clever Hansel poked an old bone between the bars instead. After weeks of this the witch grew impatient and decided to eat Hansel anyway. She instructed the terrified Gretel to prepare the oven for her brother. When the witch asked if the fire was hot enough Gretel pretended not to understand. Infuriated, the witch leaned into the oven and, quick as a flash, Gretel pushed her inside and slammed the door shut. She freed her brother and the pair found a chest full of precious stones. Filling their pockets with the treasure, the children fled back to their home where they found their father, who had been mourning the loss of his children. Their wicked stepmother had died so the three of them lived happily ever after.

Gingerbread House

Make the gingerbread at least a day before assembling the house, leaving you plenty of time to decorate.

GINGERBREAD
- 250 g (9 oz) unsalted butter
- 225 g (8 oz) dark brown sugar
- 60 ml (2 fl oz) golden syrup
- 2 tbsp black treacle
- 600 g (1 lb 5 oz) plain flour
- 2 tsp bicarbonate of soda
- 4 tsp ground ginger
- 1 tsp ground cinnamon

ICING
- 1 quantity of royal icing (see page 21)

DECORATION
- Assortment of sweets and chocolates
- Ready-made caramel, for drizzling
- Candy canes

MAKE THE GINGERBREAD

1 Preheat the oven to 200°C (400°F).

2 Melt the butter, sugar, golden syrup and black treacle in a pan and leave to cool.

3 Sift the flour, bicarbonate of soda, ginger and cinnamon into a bowl and mix well. Make a well in the flour mixture and pour in the butter mixture. Mix well, then turn out onto a floured surface and knead lightly into a smooth dough.

4 Place the dough onto a large sheet of baking parchment and roll it out to a thickness of approximately 1 cm (½ in). If you don't have a non-stick rolling pin, place another piece of baking parchment on top of the dough and roll the dough between the sheets.

5 Cut out the following panels using the templates on pages 182–184: two roof panels, two side walls, one front wall and one back wall. Using a heart cutter, cut a heart window in the front wall and cut a door freehand, using a knife. Use a large square cutter to cut windows in the side walls.

6 Place the cut pieces, still on the baking parchment, on a baking sheet and bake in the oven for 10–12 minutes, until the surface is slightly firm and no longer shiny. The gingerbread will harden once it is out of the oven, so be careful not to overbake it.

7 For the walls that have windows, you can create sugar 'glass'. Crush some boiled sweets and place them in the window spaces 5 minutes before the end of the baking time. The sweets will melt and fill the window spaces.

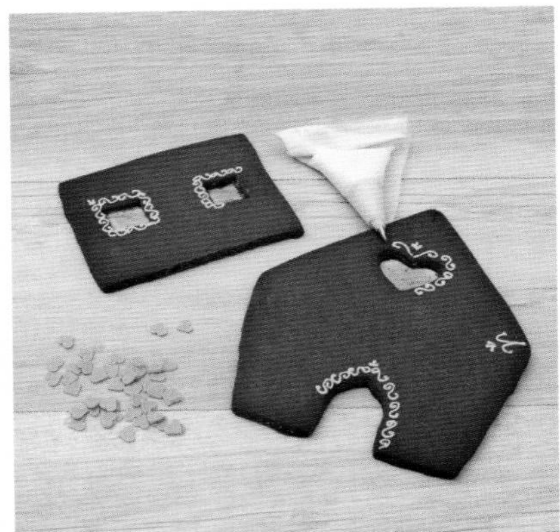

ASSEMBLE THE HOUSE

1. Allow the pieces to fully cool before you start to assemble the gingerbread house.

2. Fit a piping bag with a round tip and fill with the royal icing.

3. Place the back panel on your work surface (inside of the panel facing upward) and pipe lines along the inside of the two side edges. Attach the side panels and push down gently to join the pieces together.

4. Leave to dry for a couple of hours (you can use food tins or small bowls to support the walls while the icing dries).

5. Once dry, attach the front wall by piping along the edges of the side panels, then stand this upright and gently push the front panel to join them together. Again, leave to dry for a couple of hours using supports.

6. Finally, attach the roof panels by piping royal icing along the tops of the front, back and side walls and also along the top of one of the roof panels. Place the roof panels in position and hold for a few minutes, ensuring they don't slide down. Place supports below the roof panels to keep them in position until fully dry (ideally leave to dry overnight).

DECORATE THE HOUSE

1 Now you can start the decorating! Use an assortment of sweets and attach these with blobs of royal icing, using the photograph above as a guide.

2 You can pipe details around the windows and door by using a small round piping tip to create swirls and dots.

3 To make a tiled roof panel, attach white candy melts with royal icing in an overlapping tiled fashion.

4 To make icicles, use a medium-sized piping tip to pipe along the roof edge. Pipe a small blob of icing and, keeping the pressure on, drag it down slightly, then take the pressure off to leave a pointy edge. Make the icicles slightly different lengths for a natural look.

5 Make a winding path by placing broken pieces of chocolate in front of the house, and drizzle caramel between the pieces. Line the path with cut halves of rolled wafer biscuits and complete the front of the house with candy canes.

Trees in the Forest

Here, the cake batter is baked inside ice cream cones to create the perfect tree shape.

MAKES 10

SPONGE CAKE
225 g (8 oz) unsalted butter
225 g (8 oz) sugar
4 eggs
225 g (8 oz) self-raising flour
1 tsp vanilla extract

BUTTERCREAM
100 g (3½ oz) unsalted butter
200 g (7 oz) icing sugar
Green food colouring
2 tbsp milk

10 ice cream cones
Icing sugar, for dusting

1. Preheat the oven to 160°C (325°F).
2. Cover the top of a deep baking tray with a layer of foil and secure tightly. Poke small holes in the foil and place an ice cream cone through each hole, with the open side facing upward.
3. Cream together the butter and sugar in an electric mixer until light and fluffy – this takes 3–4 minutes.
4. Add the eggs, one at a time, along with 1 tablespoon of the flour to prevent the mixture curdling. Mix until the eggs are just incorporated, but do not overmix.
5. Add the remaining flour and fold it in, along with the vanilla extract.
6. Fill a piping bag with the cake batter and pipe into the prepared ice cream cones, filling them about two-thirds full.
7. Bake in the oven for 15–20 minutes. Remove from the oven and leave to cool in the tray for about 10 minutes.
8. Using a serrated knife, level off the tops of the cakes.
9. To make the buttercream, cream together the butter and sugar until pale and fluffy. Add a few drops of green food colouring and a splash of milk until it is a spreadable consistency (you may not need all the milk, so add a little at a time).
10. Fit a piping bag with a small star tip and fill with the buttercream. Starting at the base of the upturned ice cream cone, pipe small elongated stars along the cone. Continue all the way to the top of the cone until it is completely covered.
11. Leave to set, then finish with a light dusting of icing sugar.

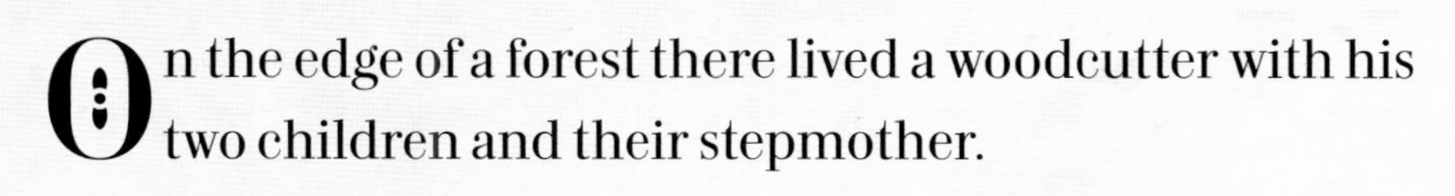

On the edge of a forest there lived a woodcutter with his two children and their stepmother.

Rocky Road

Recreate your very own rocky road from the classic tale of Hansel and Gretel.

MAKES 16 SQUARES

- 100 g (3½ oz) unsalted butter
- 200 g (7 oz) milk chocolate chips
- 100 g (3½ oz) dark chocolate chips
- 3 tbsp golden syrup
- 100 g (3½ oz) mini marshmallows
- 100 g (3½ oz) chocolate chip cookies, roughly crushed
- 100 g (3½ oz) hazelnuts, roughly chopped
- 15 g (½ oz) white chocolate, melted

1. Line a 15-cm (6-in) square tin with baking parchment.
2. Melt together the butter, milk and dark chocolate chips and golden syrup in a pan over low heat. Leave to cool slightly, for approximately 10 minutes.
3. Tip the marshmallows, cookies and nuts into the chocolate mixture and mix until well coated.
4. Pour into the prepared tin and refrigerate for 2–3 hours until set.
5. Remove from the tin and drizzle with the melted white chocolate. Cut into squares and serve.

Hansel overheard their plan and crept out of the house to gather pockets full of white pebbles... Thanks to Hansel's cunning plan they followed the trail of white pebbles home, much to their stepmother's horror.

A little house made entirely of gingerbread, with windows of clear sugar and the walls and roof covered in cakes and candy canes.

Gretel's Crunchy Chocolate Bites

Look out for mini cupcake cases to make tiny versions of these chocolate bites.

MAKES 12 LARGE OR 24 MINI

- 250 g (9 oz) milk chocolate, broken into pieces
- 50 g (1¾ oz) unsalted butter
- 2 tbsp golden syrup
- 200 g (7 oz) cereal, such as Rice Krispies or Corn Flakes
- Sprinkles or chopped nuts (optional)

1. Line a 12-hole cupcake tin or 24-hole mini cupcake tin with cupcake cases.
2. Melt the chocolate, butter and golden syrup together in a saucepan over low heat. Alternatively, you can melt these ingredients in the microwave: heat in 30-second bursts, taking care not to overheat.
3. Remove from the heat and add the cereal. Mix well until fully coated.
4. Use a teaspoon to fill the cupcake cases with the mixture and refrigerate until the chocolate has cooled and set. If you wish, you can sprinkle chopped nuts or colourful sprinkles on top before placing in the fridge.

Little Red Riding Hood

Long ago there was a little girl who lived near the dark woods. Everyone knew her as Little Red Riding Hood because she always wore a red cloak that her grandmother had made for her.

One day her mother asked her to go and visit her grandmother, who was very ill. She put some apples and a cake in her basket and set off. 'Run along now,' she said, 'and keep to the path.'

As she wandered through the woods, little did she know that she was being watched by a greedy wolf. He stepped right into the middle of the path. 'Where are you going, little girl?' he asked. 'To visit my grandmother,' replied Little Red Riding Hood politely, 'she lives just beyond those nut trees.' The cunning wolf decided that he could have not one but two tasty meals, so he quickly bounded off, straight to grandmother's cottage. He walked straight in and, with his sharp yellow teeth and eyes as bright as knives, he gobbled her up in one gulp. He then climbed into her bed, put on her nightcap, pulled the blanket over him and lay waiting for the little girl.

Before long, Little Red Riding Hood arrived at the cottage and let herself in. All was quiet and still as she approached her grandmother's bed. She pulled back the curtains from the bed.

'Oh, grandmother, what big ears you have!'

'All the better to hear you with, my dear. Come closer.'

'Oh, grandmother, what big eyes you have!'

'All the better to see you with. Come closer still.'

'But grandmother, what big teeth you have,' cried the little girl.

'All the better to EAT you with, my dear.' And with that the greedy wolf gobbled up Little Red Riding Hood and fell into a deep sleep.

Fortunately, a huntsman happened to be passing grandmother's cottage and heard the wolf's snores. When he saw the sleeping wolf he realised what had happened. He took his hunting knife and sliced through the wolf's belly. Out tumbled Little Red Riding Hood and her grandmother, glad to be alive. To punish the wolf they filled his belly with stones and stitched him up, good and tight.

Little Red Riding Hood's Basket

Fill this pretty cake basket with tasty treats, such as the Apple Cakes (see page 84). Finish by tying a ribbon around the handle.

- 1.5 kg (3 lb 5 oz) cream fondant
- 2 wooden skewers
- 1 x 20-cm (8-in) square cake (see page 15)
- 1 kg (2¼ lb) buttercream (see page 19)
- Brown food colouring paste
- Edible glue
- Small amount of royal icing (see page 21)
- Apple Cakes (see page 84)
- Ribbon

1. Make the handle of the basket first so that it has time to set. Take 250 g (9 oz) of the cream fondant and roll it into a fat sausage, around 30 cm (12 in) in length. Curve it into a handle shape and insert a wooden skewer in both ends, then set aside to dry.

2. Level the square cake layers and then fill with buttercream (see page 13). Use a serrated knife to carve the cake into a basket shape. Mark 2.5 cm (1 in) in from each corner at the base of the cake. Then cut from the top of one edge at an angle down to the marked point. Repeat on all four sides so that you have a cake that is a 15-cm (6-in) square at the base with tapered sides.

3. Create a shallow hollow in the top of the cake by leaving a 2.5-cm (1-in) border and removing the excess cake from the middle. Crumb coat the whole cake with buttercream (see page 9).

4. Roll out 115 g (4 oz) of the cream fondant to a thickness of 3 mm (⅛ in), and cut a piece the same size as the inside of the basket. Place this inside the basket.

5. Colour the remaining fondant light brown and then roll it out to a thickness of 3 mm (⅛ in). Use a basketweave-patterned rolling pin to imprint the pattern onto the fondant.

6. Measure the sides of the cake and cut a piece of fondant to the same size with an additional 5 cm (2 in) added to the height. Attach to the cake using the edible glue and fold the excess over the top of the basket and tuck inside. Repeat for all four sides.

7. Roll out two long sausages of brown fondant (this can also be done using a sugar shaper gun) and twist them together to make a long rope. Attach all the way around the top of the basket.

8. Roll two slightly thinner long sausages of brown fondant and twist together to make a long rope. Wrap around the handle using edible glue.

9. Secure the handle to the cake with some royal icing and by inserting the wooden skewers into the cake. Fill with Apple Cakes (see page 84) and finish by attaching a ribbon to the handle.

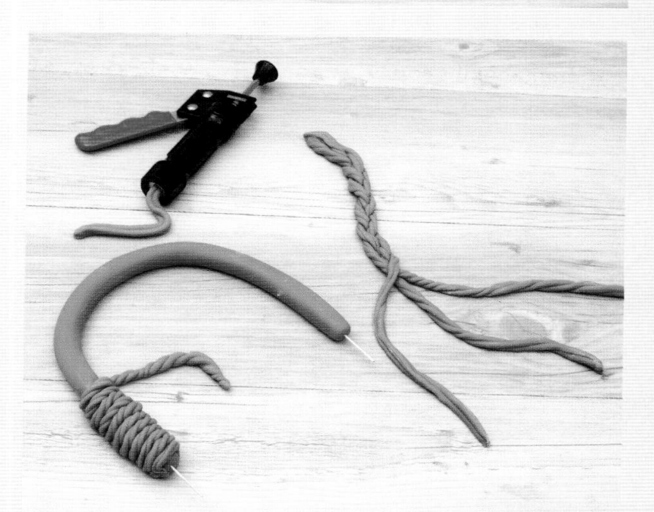

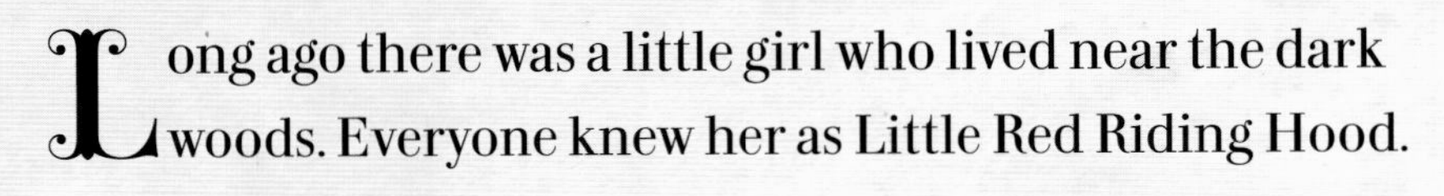

Long ago there was a little girl who lived near the dark woods. Everyone knew her as Little Red Riding Hood.

Black Forest Cupcakes

Chocolate and cherries make these cupcakes a sumptuous teatime treat.

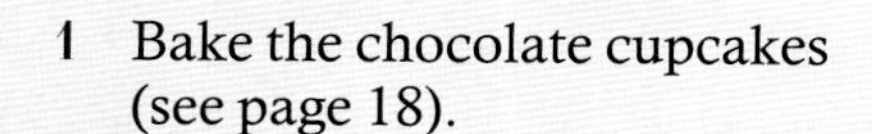

MAKES 12

12 chocolate cupcakes (see page 18)
175 g (6 oz) pitted cherries, plus 12 whole cherries for decorating
3 tbsp sugar
1 tbsp cornflour
500 g (1 lb 2 oz) buttercream (see page 19)
Chocolate shavings

1. Bake the chocolate cupcakes (see page 18).
2. As they are cooling, prepare the cherry filling. Place the pitted cherries in a saucepan over low heat until the juices start to escape, simmer for 10 minutes, then remove from the heat.
3. Mix together the sugar and cornflour and add to the cherries.
4. Return the pan to the heat and stir until the mixture thickens. Remove from the heat and leave to cool.
5. Use a teaspoon to scoop out the middle of the cupcakes and fill with the cherry mixture.
6. Pipe a swirl of buttercream on the cupcakes and drizzle over some of the remaining cherry juices. Top with chocolate shavings and cherries.

Apple Cakes

You will need 12 half-sphere silicone moulds to make these tempting apple cakes.

MAKES 6

1 quantity of 15-cm (6-in) round cake batter (see page 15)
300 g (10½ oz) buttercream (see page 19)
650 g (1½ lb) fondant
Red, green and brown food colouring pastes
Edible glue
Confectioners' glaze spray

1. Preheat the oven to 170°C (340°F). Make up the cake batter and bake in silicone half-sphere moulds for 20 minutes, or until a skewer inserted into the centre comes out clean. Leave to cool for 10–15 minutes.
2. While still in the moulds, use a serrated knife to slice off the tops of the mini cakes. Once fully cooled, use a teaspoon to scoop out a small hollow in the centre of the cakes.
3. Using a palette knife, fill the hollows with buttercream and spread buttercream along the tops of the mini cakes, making them level with the top of the mould. Chill in the fridge for 10 minutes.
4. Carefully remove half of the cakes from their moulds. Place these on top of the cakes still in the moulds, to make full spheres. Chill for a further 20 minutes and then remove all the spheres from their moulds.
5. Slice a 2.5-cm (1-in) circle from the bottom of all the cake balls, and use a knife to cut an indent from the top of the ball, to resemble an apple.
6. Wearing vinyl gloves, spread a heaped tablespoon of buttercream on the palm of your hand, then pick up a cake ball and roll it around in your hands until it is fully covered.
7. Colour all but 50 g (1¾ oz) of the fondant red and roll out to a thickness of 3 mm (⅛ in). Use to cover each cake (see page 12), taking care to push the fondant into the wedge at the top. Trim off excess fondant.
8. Make leaves by colouring 40 g (1½ oz) of fondant green and rolling it out. Use a leaf cutter to cut six leaf shapes. Attach these to the top of the apples with edible glue.
9. Colour the remaining fondant brown and roll into six stalks. Attach using edible glue.
10. Finish by spraying the apples with confectioners' glaze spray to make them shiny.

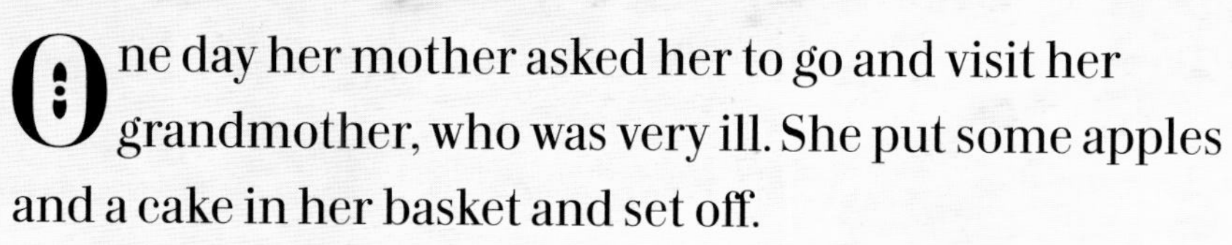

One day her mother asked her to go and visit her grandmother, who was very ill. She put some apples and a cake in her basket and set off.

Wolf Cake Pops

Like the greedy wolf, you'll be gobbling up these tasty treats in no time!

MAKES 10–15

- 1 x 10-cm (4-in) round cake (see page 15)
- 300 g (10½ oz) buttercream (see page 19)
- 10–15 cake pop sticks
- 10 g (¼ oz) white chocolate or candy melts, melted
- Black food colouring paste
- 1 tbsp (20 g) black fondant

1. Process the baked cake in a food processor until it forms crumbs.
2. Add some buttercream, a tablespoon at a time, until it starts to come together and forms a dough-like consistency.
3. Take a tablespoon of the mixture and roll it into a ball.
4. Dip a cake pop stick into the melted white chocolate or candy melts and insert it into the cake pop.
5. Add a small flattened ball of cake-pop mixture for the muzzle. Roll out two balls, pinch to make pointed ears, and attach to the top of the cake pop.
6. Place in the fridge and leave to set.
7. Meanwhile, colour the remaining buttercream grey by adding black food colouring paste, but don't mix it in uniformly – leave the colour a marbled grey/white/black mixture.
8. Use a tiny palette knife to cover the cake pop in buttercream. Use the palette knife to roughly flick up the buttercream to make it look like fur.
9. Roll three small balls of black fondant for the nose and eyes and attach these to the cake pops.

As she wandered through the woods, little did she know that she was being watched by a greedy wolf.

Snow White

As a young queen pricked her finger on a needle, three drops of blood stained the fresh snow on her black windowsill, and the queen wished with all her heart for a daughter with skin as white as snow, lips as red as blood, and hair as black as ebony. Soon after, the queen gave birth to a baby girl who fulfilled her wish. She named the baby Snow White, but the young queen passed away, leaving her daughter to the care of a new queen – beautiful, but spiteful and vain.

The new queen asked her magic mirror every morning, 'Magic mirror in my hand, who is the fairest in the land?' And every day, the mirror answered, 'My queen, you are the fairest in the land.' But by the time Snow White turned seven, she was more beautiful than her stepmother. When the magic mirror told his queen, 'My queen, you are the fairest here so true. But Snow White is a thousand times more beautiful than you,' she flew into a jealous rage.

The queen ordered a huntsman to kill Snow White, but struck by her beauty, he let her escape into the forest – never to return. Snow White discovered a tiny cottage belonging to seven dwarfs, who agreed to take her in. When the queen next consulted her magic mirror, she was horrified to hear, 'My queen, you are the fairest here so true. But beyond the mountains at the house of the seven dwarfs, Snow White is a thousand times more beautiful than you.'

The queen used the darkest of magic to create a poisoned apple. As soon as the seven dwarfs set off to work in the mine, the wicked queen disguised herself as an old woman and offered the terrible fruit to Snow White. When the princess took a bite, she slipped into a death-like sleep. Distraught, the dwarfs placed Snow White in a glass coffin. A prince travelling through the kingdom found her. Enchanted by her beauty, he fell in love and had his servants carry away the coffin. As they walked, the servants stumbled and dislodged a piece of poisoned apple inside Snow White's throat – she awoke! As the pair planned to marry, the evil queen was appalled to hear, 'You, my queen, are fair so true. But the young queen is a thousand times fairer than you.' The murderous stepmother was forced to answer for her crimes by the new king.

Snow White Cake

Prepare and bake the cake at least a day before eating and leave yourself plenty of time for the decoration. You'll also need a silicone mirror mould. (see page 187 for suppliers).

1 quantity of 18-cm (7-in) round cake batter (see page 15)
Grated zest of 2 limes
200 g (7 oz) desiccated coconut

BUTTERCREAM
200 g (7 oz) unsalted butter
500 g (1 lb 2 oz) icing sugar
Squeeze of lime juice
2–3 tbsp milk

MIRROR FRAMES
150 g (5¼ oz) white fondant
Gold and silver edible paints

SNOW WHITE FIGURE
100 g (3½ oz) white gum paste
Wooden skewer
Flesh, black, red and brown food colouring pastes
White petal dust
Rejuvenator spirit
Edible glue

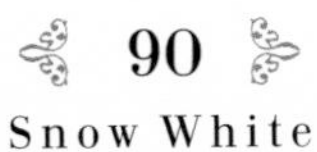

MAKE AND ASSEMBLE THE CAKE

1 Preheat the oven to 160°C (325°F) and line an 18-cm (7-in) round cake tin with baking parchment. Make the cake batter, adding the lime zest along with the flours. Bake and cool as directed (see page 15).

2 To make the buttercream, cream together the butter and icing sugar until they start to come together, then add a squeeze of lime juice to taste. Add 1 tablespoon of milk at a time, until the buttercream has a spreadable consistency.

3 Once ready to assemble, use a large serrated knife to level the top of the cake. Slice the cake into three equal layers, using a cake leveller or a large serrated knife.

4 Place the bottom layer on a cake board or plate, and spread with a layer of buttercream (using a palette knife will ensure it is evenly spread and flat). Continue layering the cakes with buttercream.

5 Once all the layers have been stacked, apply a coat of buttercream around the sides. Sprinkle the whole cake with the desiccated coconut to give it a snowy effect, tilting the cake slightly, if necessary, to cover the sides.

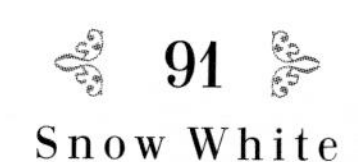

MAKE THE MIRROR FRAMES

1 Knead the fondant until soft and pliable.

2 Roll some out and push into the silicone mirror mould. Using a small palette knife, remove any excess fondant. Place the mould in the freezer for 5–10 minutes to harden – this makes it easier to remove the mirror from the mould without distorting the shape.

3 Remove from the freezer and peel back the mould, then leave the mirror to set for a few hours. Repeat this a further five times, to make six mirrors in total.

4 Once fully dry, the mirrors can be coloured. Use an edible metallic antique gold paint to colour the frame and edible silver paint for the mirror.

5 Once the paint is dry, attach the mirrors to the cake with a blob of buttercream.

MAKE THE SNOW WHITE FIGURE

1 Knead the white gum paste until soft and pliable. Roll into a sausage shape between the palms of your hands, making one side thinner than the other. Using your fingers, flatten the thicker end of the sausage to make the bottom of the skirt. Place this on top of the cake.

2 Insert a wooden skewer into the middle of the skirt, with the lower 5 cm (2 in) of the skewer inside the cake. This will give the figure some stability. Keep another 5 cm (2 in) of the skewer poking out through the top of the skirt and cut off the remainder of the skewer with kitchen scissors.

3 Colour a 40 g (1½-oz) ball of gum paste a light flesh tone using a tiny amount of paste colour, kneading well for an even colour. Cut the ball in half, wrap one half in cling film, and put it to one side, making sure it is well wrapped, since it can dry out very quickly when exposed to the air.

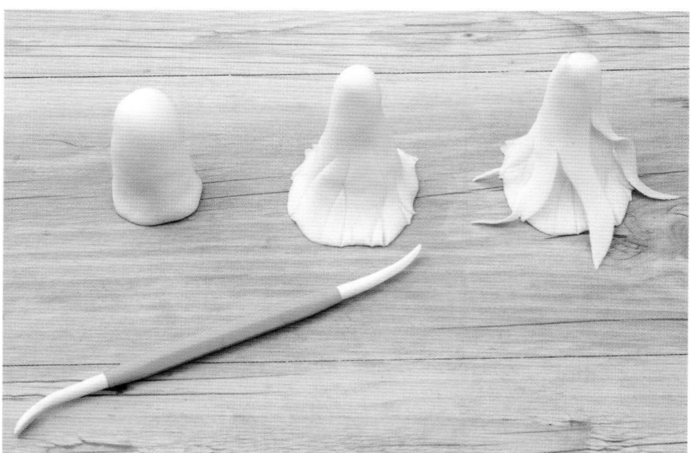

4 Using the other half, roll out another sausage and flatten it to make Snow White's body. Gently pinch one side to elongate the paste to make her neck. Attach this to the skirt with the skewer, using a tiny drop of water to stick the two pieces together.

5 Take a piece of white gum paste and roll it out very thinly. Drape around Snow White's body to make the upper part of the dress, using a drop of water to attach it. You can pleat it and drape it around her, then gather it behind her waist and cut off the excess.

6 To make her arms, roll two sausages from the flesh-coloured gum paste. Flatten one side and make four small incisions in the paste. Gently twist to make her fingers. Repeat with the other arm.

7 Bend the arms using a toothpick to make the crease and attach the arms to the sides of her body. Place a small support in front of the body to rest the arms on while they set.

8 Using the remaining flesh-coloured gum paste, roll a ball for her head. Shape a nose by pinching the paste, and make two tiny holes by inserting a toothpick. Roll out tiny, thin sausages of gum paste and shape them into lips. Smooth the edges to blend them onto her face.

9 Make a white paste by mixing some white petal dust with a few drops of rejuvenator spirit. Use this to paint her eyes. Complete the eyes using black gum paste for her eyelashes and pupils, and paint her lips red. Attach the head to the body using a toothpick and a dab of edible glue.

10 For the hair, colour some gum paste black and roll it out thinly. Cut strips of paste and score with lines using a knife. Attach these to her head and gently twist the ends to make it look more natural.

11 Make some apples using red gum paste. Roll out small balls and shape them into apples. Insert a tiny stalk by rolling a small piece of brown gum paste. Place one apple in her hand, using a small drop of water to stick it on.

Red Lips Cookies

Make these at least 24 hours before you want to eat them to allow time for them to set.

MAKES 20–25

1 quantity of cookie dough (see page 18)
Lip-shaped cookie cutter

ROYAL ICING

2 level tbsp (30 g) powdered egg white
110 ml (3¾ fl oz) warm water
¼ tsp cream of tartar
600 g (1 lb 5 oz) icing sugar
Red food colouring paste
Red-coloured sugar (optional)

1. Make the cookie dough and chill in the fridge for 15–30 minutes.
2. Roll the dough out onto a floured surface to a thickness of 5 mm (¼ in).
3. Using a lip-shaped cookie cutter, cut out the cookie shapes and place them on a baking sheet lined with baking parchment. Chill in the fridge for 30 minutes – this will ensure the cookies stay flat and don't spread during baking. Preheat the oven to 180°C (350°F).
4. Bake for 7–8 minutes, until they stop looking wet on the surface. They will still be soft at this stage but do not overbake – they will continue to harden when removed from the oven. Leave to cool completely before decorating.
5. To make the royal icing, use an electric stand mixer to mix the powdered egg white with the water and cream of tartar until just incorporated.
6. Add the icing sugar and mix on low speed for approximately 5 minutes. Colour the royal icing with red food colouring paste.
7. Fit a piping bag with a small round tip, fill with some of the red royal icing and pipe an outline around the edge of the cookies.
8. Add a few drops of water to the remaining royal icing and mix until you get a slightly thinner consistency. If the icing is too runny, add more icing sugar to thicken it. Once you have the right consistency, fill up a piping bag or a squeezy bottle and flood the cookies up to the outlines (see page 12).
9. If you wish, sprinkle red-coloured sugar onto the lips to make them sparkle. Allow to harden and set for 24 hours.

The queen wished with all her heart for a daughter with skin as white as snow, lips as red as blood, and hair as black as ebony.

As soon as the seven dwarfs set off to work in the mine, the wicked queen disguised herself as an old woman.

Dwarf Hat Cake Pops

You can also make these pops using leftover cake from other bakes.

MAKES 15–20

SPONGE CAKE
115 g (4 oz) unsalted butter
115 g (4 oz) sugar
2 eggs
½ tsp vanilla extract
115 g (4 oz) self-raising flour

BUTTERCREAM
300 g (10½ oz) buttercream (see page 19), flavoured with ½ tsp vanilla extract

DECORATION
100 g (3½ oz) white chocolate or candy melts
15–20 cake pop sticks
80 g (2¾ oz) red candy melts

1. Preheat the oven to 160°C (325°F) and line a 15-cm (6-in) round cake tin with baking parchment.
2. Cream together the butter and sugar until light and fluffy – this takes 3–4 minutes.
3. Add the eggs one at a time to the butter mixture, along with the vanilla extract and 1 tablespoon of the flour. Stir until the eggs are just combined; don't overmix. Add the remaining flour and fold it in.
4. Transfer to the prepared tin and bake for 25–30 minutes or until the top is pale golden brown and springs back when touched. Insert a skewer to check the inside – it should come out clean with a few crumbs attached.
5. Remove from the oven and leave to cool in the tin for 10 minutes, then remove from the tin and leave to cool fully. Place the cooled cake in a food processor and blitz until it resembles crumbs.
6. Add buttercream, a tablespoon at a time, and mix until the mixture starts to stick together and hold its shape.
7. Place the white chocolate or white candy melts in a heatproof bowl and melt in the microwave in short bursts, stirring often.
8. Take some of the cake mixture in your hand and shape it into a dwarf's hat. Dip the end of a cake pop stick into the white chocolate or candy melts, then insert it into the bottom of the hat. Rest on a baking sheet while you repeat with the remaining cake mixture. Refrigerate for 20 minutes. Once chilled, the cake pop sticks should stay firmly in place.
9. Dip the whole dwarf hat into the white chocolate or candy melts, then refrigerate to set while you melt the red candy melts in a separate bowl.
10. Once set, dip the hats into the melted red candy melts, leaving a rim of white showing at the brim of the hat. Place in the fridge again to set.

Candy Apples

These striking red treats are sticky and sweet, and oh so easy to make.

MAKES 8

100 ml (3½ fl oz) golden syrup
200 ml (7 fl oz) water
250 g (9 oz) sugar
¼ tsp cream of tartar
8 apples, washed
8 cake pop sticks
Red and black food colouring

1. Place the golden syrup, water, sugar and cream of tartar in a saucepan and bring to a boil over medium heat.
2. While the mixture is heating, remove the stems from the washed apples and insert the cake pop sticks.
3. Using a candy thermometer, boil the mixture to 150°C (300°F) – the bubbles will become smaller and closer together. Once it has reached the correct temperature, take the saucepan off the heat and add a few drops of red food colouring.
4. Dip the apples one by one to coat all over, then place them on a piece of baking parchment to set.
5. Once all the apples have been dipped, add a few drops of black food colouring to darken the remaining mixture (it may need to be reheated, since it sets very quickly). Using a spoon, drop some of the darker mixture over the tops of the apples and allow it to drip down the sides. Leave to set and harden before serving.

The queen used the darkest of magic to create a poisoned apple, and in disguise, offered the terrible fruit to Snow White. When the princess took a bite, she slipped into a death-like sleep.

The Princess and the Pea

Once upon a time there was a prince who wanted to marry; but she would have to be a real princess. He travelled all over the world to find one, but nowhere could he find what he wanted. He met many beautiful and rich girls who all claimed to be real princesses but there was always something about them that was not as it should be. So he came home and was sad, for he longed to marry a real princess.

One evening, a terrible storm came on; there was thunder and lightning, and the rain poured down in torrents. Suddenly, a knocking was heard at the palace gate and the old queen ordered the servants to open it.

There was a girl standing in front of the gate. She was beautiful to look at but, good gracious! What a sight the rain and the wind had made her look. The water ran down from her hair and clothes; it ran down into the toes of her shoes and out again at the heels. And yet she said that she was a real princess.

The prince was struck by her beauty. 'We'll soon find out if she is a real princess,' said the queen. While the servants tended to the girl and found her dry clothes and fed her, the queen went to the bedroom and laid a tiny pea under the mattress. She then ordered the servants to place twenty mattresses on top of the bed, and twenty eiderdowns on top of the mattresses.

When night fell the queen showed the girl to her bedroom and bade her good night. 'Sleep well, my dear,' she said.

'Thank you, I shall,' replied the girl. But as soon as she lay on the bed she found she could not sleep, for she was very uncomfortable. The next morning the queen asked her how she had slept.

'Oh, very badly!' said she. 'I have scarcely closed my eyes all night. Heaven only knows what was in the bed, but I was lying on something hard, so that I am black and blue all over my body. It's horrible!'

Then they knew that she was a real princess because she had felt the pea right through the twenty mattresses and the twenty eiderdowns. Only a real princess could be as sensitive as that. So the prince took her for his wife. As for the pea, it was put on display in a glass cabinet in a museum, where it may still be seen today.

Mattress Cake

Don't forget to add the hidden pea under all those mattresses!

- 1 x 20-cm (8-in) square cake (see page 15)
- 1 kg (2¼ lb) buttercream (see page 19)
- 150 g (5¼ oz) fondant
- 50 g (1¾ oz) gum paste
- Pink, lilac, yellow, green and blue food colouring pastes
- Edible glue

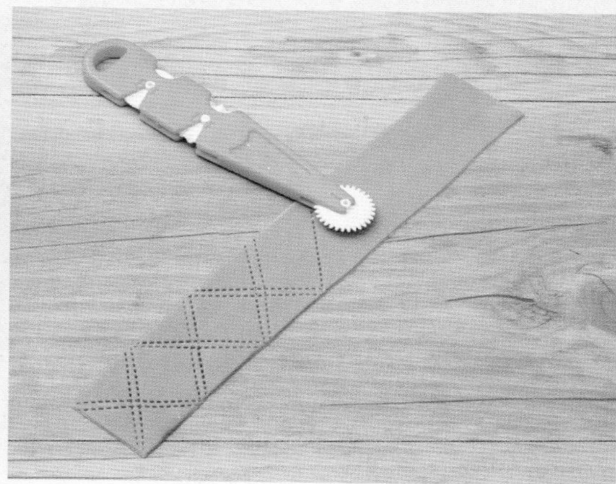

1 Let the cake layers cool fully, then, using a serrated knife, level the tops of the layers and cut in half, so you have four layers that are 10 cm (4 in) wide. Then slice 5 cm (2 in) off the ends of the cakes to make four 10 x 15-cm (4 x 6-in) layers. Stack and fill the layers with buttercream to make a double-height cake (see page 13).

2 Crumb coat the entire cake (see page 9).

3 Starting at the bottom, create a different mattress for each layer. Using the photograph as a guide, colour small amounts of fondant for the mattresses, and gum paste for the mattress frills.

4 Roll out a strip of white fondant 2.5 cm (1 in) wide and 50 cm (20 in) long. Thinly roll out pink gum paste or fondant and cut out small circles using a circle cutter. Attach to the white fondant in a polka-dot pattern using edible glue. Wrap this around the base of the cake to make the first mattress layer.

5 Roll out strips in lilac, yellow, pink and green-coloured gum paste to the same dimensions as the first mattress.

6 For the lilac strip, use a quilting tool to emboss diagonal lines of stitches. For the pink strip, use a texture mat to emboss a pattern in the paste. Attach all these strips to the cake, one above the other.

7 Thinly roll out green, light blue and dark blue-coloured gum paste, then use a garrett frill cutter to cut a piece 50 cm (20 in) long from each colour. Use the conical-shaped tool to frill the edges. Straighten out the frills and attach to the cake in between mattresses.

8 Roll a small ball of green gum paste and attach this inside the frill of the light blue mattress to resemble the pea.

9 For the top of the cake, roll out a large piece of fondant about 5 cm (2 in) wider than the cake. Cover the top of the cake with this, draping it along the sides, then use a sharp knife to trim the excess fondant.

10 Use a cutting wheel to make diagonal lines on the top of the mattress. Use a toothpick to indent holes where the diagonal lines meet.

11 Use a sugar gun to squeeze out long, thin sausages of gum paste to match each of the mattress colours (or you can roll these by hand). Attach these to the top edge of the mattresses.

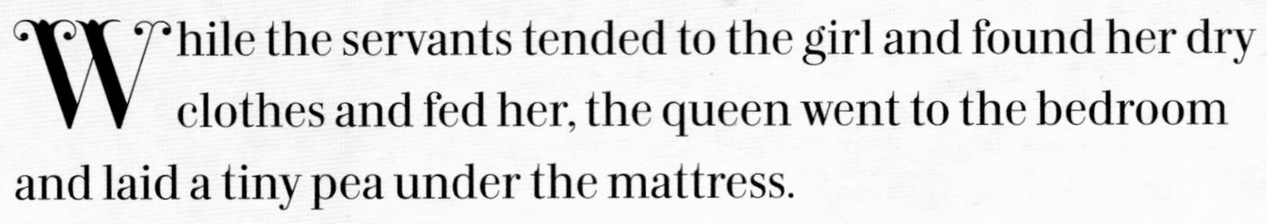

While the servants tended to the girl and found her dry clothes and fed her, the queen went to the bedroom and laid a tiny pea under the mattress.

Hidden Pea Cupcakes

When you slice these delightful cupcakes in half, you will see the hidden pea inside.

MAKES 12

1 quantity of 10-cm (4-in) round cake batter, for the hidden peas (see page 15)
500 g (1 lb 2 oz) buttercream (see page 19)
Dark green food colouring paste
1 quantity of 15-cm (6-in) round cake batter, for the cupcakes (see page 15)

1. Mix the batter for the 10-cm (4-in) cake and bake for 20–25 minutes until golden brown. Leave to cool, then process the cake in a food processor until it resembles crumbs.
2. Add a tablespoon of the buttercream at a time to the crumbs, until they start to stick together and resemble cake pop mixture. Colour this mixture dark green.
3. Roll 12 balls of green cake pops about 2.5 cm (1 in) in diameter, then freeze for 2–3 hours or overnight.
4. Preheat the oven to 170°C (340°F). Line a 12-cup cupcake tin with cupcake cases.
5. Mix the batter for the cupcakes and then spoon 1 tablespoon of cake batter into the base of each case.
6. Place a frozen cake pop ball into each case and spoon the remaining cake batter on top, fully covering the cake pops, until the cases are about two-thirds full.
7. Bake for approximately 20 minutes, until the cupcakes are springy to touch. Leave to cool fully on a wire cooling rack.
8. Use green food colouring paste to tint the remaining buttercream pale green.
9. Fill a piping bag fitted with a round tip and pipe blobs all over the cupcakes.

Feather Cupcakes

Make the feathers first to allow them sufficient time to dry – at least 4–6 hours.

MAKES 12

50 g (1¾ oz) white gum paste
12 cupcakes (see page 16)
500 g (1 lb 2 oz) buttercream (see page 19)
Pink food colouring paste

MAKE THE FEATHERS

1. Thinly roll out a piece of white gum paste. Working freehand, cut out a feather outline roughly 7.5 cm (3 in) long, using a cutting wheel.
2. Continuing with the cutting wheel, make a mid-line by rolling down the middle of the feather shape, but not cutting all the way through.
3. Move the cutting wheel from the mid-line to the edge of the feather several times along the length of the feather, taking care not to put too much pressure on it as you only want to indent.
4. Apply more pressure as you move the cutting wheel across the edge of the feather, about 1 cm (½ in) in from the edge, to cut through the paste and create a feathered edge all the way around.
5. Place on a foam drying tray across the ridges to dry the feather in a natural curved shape. Make 12 feathers in total.

ASSEMBLE THE CUPCAKES

1. Bake the cupcakes (see page 16). Leave to cool fully on a wire cooling rack.
2. Make the buttercream and colour it a very light pink. Spoon into a piping bag fitted with a star tip and use to pipe swirls on top of each cupcake.
3. Place the dried feathers on top of each swirl of buttercream.

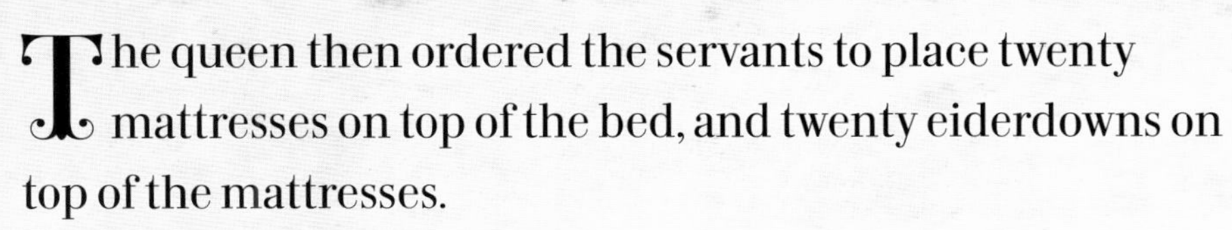

The queen then ordered the servants to place twenty mattresses on top of the bed, and twenty eiderdowns on top of the mattresses.

Pea Tart

You will need six mini tart tins for this recipe, each 7.5 cm (3 in) in diameter.

MAKES 6

PASTRY
200 g (7 oz) plain flour
50 g (1¾ oz) icing sugar
Pinch of salt
100 g (3½ oz) unsalted butter, diced
1 egg yolk
1–2 tbsp cold milk

CRÈME PÂTISSIÈRE
225 ml (7½ fl oz) milk
½ tsp vanilla extract
3 egg yolks
50 g (1¾ oz) sugar
1 tbsp plain flour
1 tbsp cornflour
Green food colouring paste

DECORATION
20 g (¾ oz) green gum paste

1. Sift the flour, sugar and salt into a bowl. Add the diced butter and cut in until the mixture resembles sand.
2. Make a well in the centre, then add the egg yolk and mix until it starts to come together. Add a tablespoon of milk at a time to form a dough. Turn out onto a floured surface and knead for 2 minutes, then chill for 20 minutes. Preheat the oven to 180°C (350°F).
3. Divide the dough into six equal pieces. Roll each out to a thickness of 5 mm (¼ in), making sure they are larger than the tart tins.
4. Place the dough into the tart tins, making sure you push it into the corners, then prick the bases with a fork. Line the tarts with baking parchment and fill with baking beans.
5. Bake for 12–15 minutes until light golden brown. Remove the baking beans and paper, and bake for a further 10 minutes.
6. Make the crème pâtissière by placing the milk and vanilla in a large saucepan and warming over low heat.
7. Place the egg yolks and sugar in a bowl and whisk until pale and creamy. Then add the flour and cornflour and continue to whisk until fully incorporated.
8. Add green food colouring and the warm milk mixture in a slow, steady stream while whisking, then return the mixture to the pan.
9. Cook over low heat, stirring continuously, until the mixture thickens. Remove from the heat and place a piece of cling film directly on the surface to avoid a film forming while it cools.
10. Once it has cooled, pour into the prepared pastry cases and leave to cool fully.
11. Roll 18 small balls of gum paste to resemble peas. Arrange these on top of the tarts.

The pea was put on display in a glass cabinet in a museum, where it may still be seen today.

Rapunzel

Long ago, a man and his wife lived in a cottage that overlooked a beautiful garden belonging to a witch. They would sit and gaze at the garden. 'If only we had a child,' they said, 'we would be truly happy.'

One day the wife saw some beautiful blue rapunzel flowers in the garden and begged her husband to fetch them for her. 'I must have those flowers to eat!' So that night the husband climbed over the wall.

'What are you doing in my garden?' The man froze. There was the witch, right in front of him. He begged her to forgive him and she agreed to let him go. 'Take the flowers,' she said, 'and when your wife gives birth to the child growing inside her, you must give her to me.'

Bewildered and excited, the man agreed and hurried home to his wife. Nine months later, the couple were overjoyed when their daughter was born. The only name they could think of to give her was Rapunzel. But their joy turned to despair when the witch arrived to take her away.

When she was twelve years old, Rapunzel was so beautiful that the witch, fearful that she would be stolen away from her, decided to lock her in a tall tower with no door. Every day she brought food for her and stood at the base of the tower.

'Rapunzel, Rapunzel, let down your hair,' she called. Rapunzel leaned out of the tower and let her long golden plait fall to the ground so the witch could climb up the tower. And so she lived, with nothing to do except daydream and sing. One day a young prince was riding through the forest and heard her beautiful voice. Coming across the tower, he spied the witch and saw her climbing up the rope of hair. The next day he returned, determined to see the owner of that beautiful voice. 'Rapunzel, Rapunzel, let down your hair.' So began the first of many visits, during which Rapunzel and the prince fell in love. But Rapunzel soon let slip that she had been seeing the prince and the furious witch cut off her plait and banished her to the forest. The witch tied the plait to a hook and waited for the prince's next visit. As he reached the top of the tower the witch cut him down and he fell into a bush of thorns, blinding his eyes. He wandered through the wilderness for many days until finally he heard a sweet voice singing. Rapunzel and the prince were reunited and her tears of joy washed his eyes so he could see again.

Rapunzel's Tower

Dusting the tower with petal dusts will really highlight the bricks and give the tower an eerie feel.

- 1 quantity of 15-cm (6-in) round cake batter (see page 15)
- 400 g (14 oz) buttercream (see page 19)
- 1 long cake dowel or wooden skewer
- 700 g (1½ lb) fondant
- Yellow, black, pink, orange and green food colouring pastes
- Brown and black petal dusts
- Large waffle cone
- Edible glue
- Small amount of royal icing

1 Preheat the oven to 160°C (325°F) and line three 7.5-cm (3-in) round cake tins with baking parchment.

2 Split the cake batter equally between the three cake tins and bake for 20–30 minutes, until the cakes turn light golden brown and a skewer inserted into the centre comes out clean.

3 Leave to cool, then, using a serrated knife, slice off the domed tops and split the cakes in half.

4 Layer the cakes with buttercream and stack to form a tall tower (see page 13). You may need to insert a long dowel or wooden skewer through the middle for support, so it stays in position. Crumb coat the tower with buttercream (see page 9).

5 Colour 500 g (1 lb 2 oz) of the fondant yellow and roll out to a thickness of 3 mm (⅛ in). Imprint with a brick-textured mat. Lay this on the work surface, embossed-side facing down.

6 Measure the height and circumference of the tower cake, then cut the fondant to the same dimensions. Lay the tower on its side on the fondant and gently roll it along, so that the cake picks up the fondant. Where the two ends of the fondant meet, gently rub the seam together, then position the tower upright.

7 Use a sharp knife to cut out a window shape near the top of the tower. Colour a small amount of fondant black and then use this cut piece to cut a piece of thinly rolled black fondant to the same size, then attach inside the window.

8 Colour about 40 g (1½ oz) of the fondant grey. Roll out to a 1-cm (½-in) thick sausage and use cake smoothers to flatten it into a more rectangular shape. Use a knife to cut pieces the same circumference as the window and then use the knife to score the fondant halfway through at varying lengths to give the impression of bricks. Use black petal dust to create shadows and highlight the grooves in the bricks and then attach around the window.

9 Roll out about 40 g (1½ oz) of white fondant to a thickness of 3 mm (⅛ in) and use to cover the waffle cone. Colour some fondant pink and some orange and roll out different-sized balls. Attach to the waffle cone with edible glue and push down to create flattened tiles. Arrange all over the waffle cone in a random fashion. Place the waffle cone on top of the tower and secure with royal icing.

10 Use brown petal dust to create shadows and highlight grooves in the bricks around the tower.

11 Colour some fondant two different shades of green and cut out tiny leaves using a leaf cutter. Arrange these on the tower, using edible glue to attach them.

12 Colour about 20 g (¾ oz) of fondant dark yellow to make Rapunzel's hair – use a sugar gun or roll out two long pieces of fondant and twist them together. Attach to the inside of the window and allow it to wind down the cake. Attach at intervals to the tower with edible glue to give the hair some support, and wind the rest around the base of the cake.

Golden Syrup-Dipped Cupcakes

These simple cupcakes are beautifully finished with a swirl of buttercream and a drizzle of golden syrup.

MAKES 12

- 175 g (6 oz) unsalted butter
- 125 g (4½ oz) sugar
- 175 g (6 oz) self-raising flour
- 3 eggs
- 3 tbsp golden syrup or honey, plus extra for drizzling
- 500 g (1 lb 2 oz) buttercream (see page 19)

1. Preheat the oven to 170°C (340°F) and line a 12-hole cupcake tin with cupcake cases.
2. Cream together the butter and sugar for a few minutes until pale and creamy.
3. Sift the flour into a separate bowl.
4. Add the eggs to the butter mixture, one at a time, along with a spoonful of flour to prevent the mixture curdling. Once all the eggs are mixed in, fold in the remaining flour.
5. Add the golden syrup or honey and mix well.
6. Spoon into the cupcake cases. Bake for approximately 20 minutes.
7. Once baked, leave to cool in the pan for 10 minutes, then remove and fully cool on a wire cooling rack.
8. Fit a piping bag with a star tip and fill with the buttercream, then pipe swirls on the cupcakes.
9. Finish by drizzling with a little golden syrup or honey.

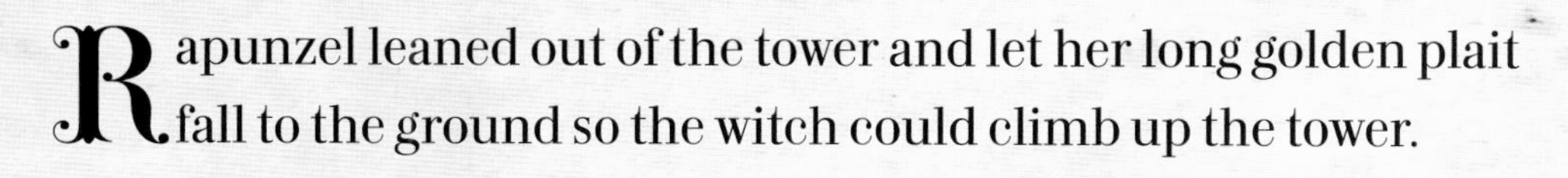

Rapunzel leaned out of the tower and let her long golden plait fall to the ground so the witch could climb up the tower.

Rapunzel and the prince fell in love. But Rapunzel soon let slip that she had been seeing the prince and the furious witch cut off her plait and banished her to the forest.

Plaited Pretzel

The cinnamon sugar dusting adds a lovely sweet note to this simple pretzel.

PRETZEL

250 ml (8½ fl oz) warm milk
2 tbsp light brown sugar
7 g (¼ oz) packet active dry yeast
400 g (14 oz) plain flour, plus extra for dusting
Pinch of salt
100 g (3½ oz) unsalted butter, melted, plus 2 tbsp for brushing
1 tbsp vegetable oil, plus extra for greasing

TOPPING

100 g (3½ oz) sugar
2 tsp ground cinnamon
1 tbsp melted butter

1. Combine the milk and sugar in the bowl of a stand mixer and sprinkle the yeast on top. Leave to sit for 10–15 minutes until the yeast blooms.
2. Add the flour, salt and butter and, using the dough hook attachment, mix on low speed until well combined. Continue mixing and kneading until the dough is fully combined and starts to become elastic. Remove from the bowl.
3. Pour the oil into the bowl and, using a pastry brush, coat the inside of the bowl well.
4. Return the dough to the bowl, cover with cling film and leave to rest in a warm place for about 1 hour for the dough to rise and double in size.
5. Preheat the oven to 220°C (425°F). Line a baking sheet with baking parchment and lightly brush with a little oil.
6. Turn the dough out onto a floured surface and divide it into three equal pieces. Roll out each piece into a long length, then join the pieces together at one end.
7. Plait the full length of the dough, joining the pieces together again at the other end. Place on the prepared baking sheet, cover with cling film and leave to rise for 30–40 minutes.
8. Remove the cling film and bake for 30–40 minutes. Check halfway through the baking time and cover with aluminium foil if it looks like it is browning too much.
9. Meanwhile, mix together the sugar and cinnamon. Once baked, remove the pretzel from the oven and brush with the melted butter. Sprinkle the cinnamon sugar on top. Leave to cool on the baking sheet for 15 minutes, then transfer to a wire cooling rack to cool completely.

Chocolate Shortbread Thorns

Shortbread is so easy to make and this chocolate version makes a delicious treat.

MAKES 12–15
200 g (7 oz) unsalted butter, softened
100 g (3½ oz) light brown sugar
225 g (8 oz) plain flour
3 tbsp cocoa powder

1. Beat together the butter and sugar until pale and creamy.
2. Sift together the flour and cocoa powder, then add to the butter and sugar mixture. Mix well until it forms a dough.
3. Roll it out to a thickness of about 2.5 cm (1 in). Alternatively, you could fill a round 15-cm (6-in) cake tin with the dough and push a cake board on top to flatten it.
4. Wrap in cling film and chill in the fridge for at least 1 hour.
5. Preheat the oven to 180°C (350°F). Line a baking sheet with baking parchment.
6. Remove the dough from the fridge and use a sharp knife to slice into triangular wedges. Use a fork to prick all over the surface and crimp the edges.
7. Transfer to the prepared baking sheet and bake for 10–12 minutes, or until firm – check by lightly pressing with a finger.
8. Remove and transfer to a wire cooling rack to fully cool.

As the prince reached the top of the tower, the witch cut him down and he fell into a bush of thorns, blinding his eyes.

The Snow Queen

Once upon a time there lived a wicked goblin who built a magic mirror. Anything that was beautiful or good was reflected in it as ugly and bad. One day, the mirror broke and its pieces fell over the earth. A few pieces fell in a town where two friends named Kay and Gerda lived.

Kay and Gerda were very good friends and spent their days playing games and running across the fields. One day, while they were playing, a piece of the broken mirror hit Kay's eyes and another pierced his heart. After that everything changed. Kay no longer treated Gerda as his best friend. He poked fun at her and was cruel to her. Gerda was puzzled and couldn't understand why he was behaving in such a strange way.

One day, Kay decided to go on a sleigh ride over the snow. Suddenly, a huge sleigh drew up before him and its driver asked him to step in. Once Kay was inside, the driver transformed himself into a woman and sped away. She was draped in a white flowing gown and on her head was a crown made of ice. Her silky white locks cascaded like a flowing stream. Astonished, Kay asked her who she was. 'I am the Snow Queen,' replied the woman, whose face shone like a sparkling diamond. She tugged at the reins and rode into the sky, until they reached a distant land.

Meanwhile, Gerda waited for Kay to return. Finally, she took her boat and went to search for him in the river. A fairy took pity on her and sent magic flowers out to search for Kay, but they returned empty-handed.

Gerda sat under a tree and wept all night. Suddenly, a crow flew down and told her about a certain princess who had recently married a boy. Gerda grew restless thinking that Kay had married someone else and urged the crow to take her to the princess's palace. Gerda waited anxiously but when the boy entered she sighed with relief because it wasn't Kay.

Gerda's search took her as far as Lapland. There, she came across a magician who told her that Kay was at the Snow Queen's palace and that because of the piece of glass inside him, he considered it to be the best place in the world. The Snow Queen's palace was made out of ice and no one except the Snow Queen lived in it. One day, she challenged Kay to spell the word 'eternity' in return for his freedom. Kay wracked his brains but just couldn't spell the word. Just then Gerda arrived, and seeing her long-lost friend, she cried out in joy and embraced him. As her warm tears fell on his cheeks Kay felt his cold heart begin to melt. He recognised Gerda and wept aloud. Kay was set free and he returned home with Gerda.

Glass Shard Cake

This simple cake is decorated with buttercream in varying shades of blue and topped with shards of sugar 'glass'.

CAKE

1 x 18-cm (7-in) round cake (see page 15)
1 kg (2¼ lb) buttercream (see page 19)
Blue food colouring paste
Cooking oil spray

SUGAR GLASS DECORATION

600 g (1 lb 5 oz) sugar
330 ml (11¼ fl oz) golden syrup
350 ml (11¾ fl oz) water
¼ tsp cream of tartar

PREPARE THE CAKE

1 Level the cake layers and use about half of the buttercream to fill and crumb coat the cake (see pages 9 and 13).

2 You need to colour the remaining buttercream in varying shades of blue. Start by colouring the entire batch in pale blue using colouring paste.

3 Place approximately one-quarter of the buttercream in a separate bowl and cover with cling film to prevent it drying out.

4 Add more paste colour to the larger bowl of buttercream to darken the shade of blue, then transfer another quarter of the buttercream into a separate bowl and cover with cling film.

5 Repeat this twice more, so you have a total of four shades of blue buttercream.

6 Fit a piping bag with a large round tip and fill it with the darkest shade of buttercream. Starting at the base of the cake, pipe a medium-sized blob of buttercream on the cake. Place a palette knife halfway on the piped buttercream, push down and drag the buttercream across to create a smear.

7 Pipe another blob next to the smear and repeat the action. Continue this all around the cake, then continue to pipe and drag for the next row using the same colour.

8 Use the next shade of buttercream for the third and fourth rows, and continue piping the buttercream with lighter shades until you reach the top of the cake.

9 For the top of the cake, use the lightest shade of buttercream and repeat the same action in a spiral pattern until you reach the middle of the cake. Set the cake aside while you prepare the glass shards.

MAKE THE SHARDS

1 Mix all the sugar glass ingredients in a saucepan and melt over low heat. Bring to a boil slowly – this will take at least 20 minutes. If you heat the mixture too fast, it will caramelise and turn brown and cloudy.

2 In the meantime, cover a baking sheet with foil and lightly spray with cooking oil.

3 Bring the temperature of the sugar mixture up to 150°C (300°F) – check using a candy thermometer or drop some of the sugar mixture into a glass of cold water, using a teaspoon. At the correct temperature it should immediately turn into hard brittle threads that break when bent. Then, working quickly, pour it onto the prepared baking sheet and leave to cool.

4 After 1 hour or so, the sugar glass should be completely set and cooled. Smash some shards of sugar glass and arrange the larger pieces in a random fashion on top of the cake. Do this just before serving the cake, since sugar glass will start to absorb moisture and soften as soon as it is placed on the cake.

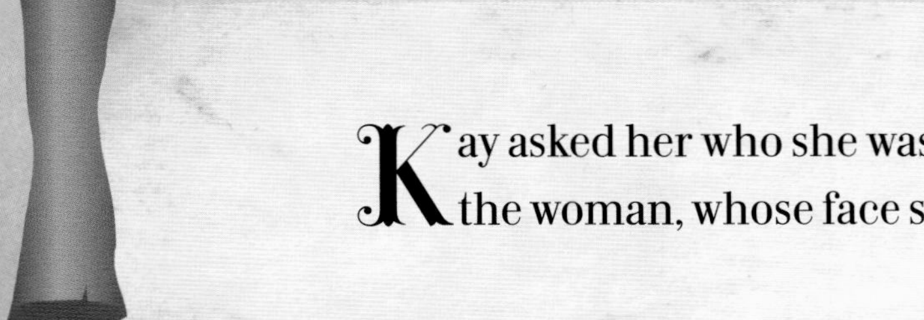

Kay asked her who she was. 'I am the Snow Queen,' replied the woman, whose face shone like a sparkling diamond.

Snowball Cakes

You will need 12 silicone half-sphere moulds for these cakes.

MAKES 6

1 quantity of 15-cm (6-in) round cake batter (see page 15)
400 g (14 oz) buttercream (see page 19)
150 g (5¼ oz) desiccated coconut

1. Preheat the oven to 170°C (340°F). Make up the cake batter and bake in 12 silicone half-sphere moulds for approximately 20 minutes, or until a skewer inserted into the centre comes out clean.
2. Remove from the oven and leave to cool for 10–15 minutes.
3. While still in the moulds, use a serrated knife to slice off the tops of the mini cakes.
4. Once fully cooled, use a small teaspoon to scoop out a small hollow in the centre of the cakes.
5. Using a palette knife, fill the small hollows with buttercream and spread buttercream along the tops of the mini cakes so that they are flush with the tops of the moulds. Place in the fridge for 10 minutes.
6. Take one half-sphere and place it on top of another half to make it a full sphere. Once all the spheres have been put together, place in the fridge for a further 20 minutes.
7. Remove from the fridge and remove all balls from the moulds.
8. Wearing vinyl gloves, spread a heaped tablespoon of buttercream on the palm of your hand, then pick up a cake ball and roll it around in your hands until it is fully covered with buttercream.
9. Dip each cake ball into a bowl of desiccated coconut to complete the snowy look.

Snowflake Cookies

Use a piping bag fitted with a fine tip so you can add lots of creative details to these snowflake cookies.

MAKES 20–25

1 quantity of cookie dough (see page 18)
250 g (9 oz) white royal icing (see page 21)
Blue food colouring paste

1. Make the cookie dough and chill in the fridge for 15–30 minutes. Line a baking sheet with baking parchment.
2. Roll the dough out onto a floured surface to a thickness of 5 mm (¼ in).
3. Using snowflake cookie cutters, cut out the cookie shapes and place the cut cookies on the lined baking sheet. For the larger cookie shapes, you can use smaller cutters to create patterns in the cookies.
4. Chill in the fridge for 30 minutes before baking in the oven. This will ensure the cookies don't spread and will stay flat to allow for easy decorating. Preheat the oven to 180°C (350°F).
5. Bake for 7–8 minutes, until they stop looking wet on the surface. They will still be soft at this stage but do not overbake, since they will continue to harden when removed from the oven. Leave to cool completely before decorating.
6. Set 2 tablespoons of the white royal icing to one side and colour the remainder pale blue. Pipe an outline using pale blue royal icing and then add a few drops of water to the rest of the blue icing to make it slightly thinner. Use this to flood the cookies (see page 12).
7. Once fully set, pipe details on the cookies using the reserved white royal icing.

The Snow Queen was draped in a white flowing gown and on her head was a crown made of ice.

The Snow Queen's palace was made out of ice and no one except the Snow Queen lived in it.

Frozen Cheesecake in a Jar

You will need six small glass jars in which to prepare and serve this cheesecake.

MAKES 6

200 g (7 oz) digestive biscuits
100 g (3½ oz) unsalted butter, melted
500 g (1 lb 2 oz) cream cheese
100 g (3½ oz) icing sugar, plus extra for dusting
250 ml (8½ fl oz) double cream
1 tsp vanilla extract
200 g (7 oz) blueberries, plus extra to decorate
50 g (1¾ oz) sugar
3–4 tbsp water
1 tbsp lemon juice

1. Place the digestive biscuits in a plastic freezer bag and crush using a rolling pin.
2. Melt the butter in a small pan, then add the crushed biscuits and mix well until the crumbs are fully coated.
3. Divide the biscuit mixture between the jars and push firmly to create an even layer for the base of the cheesecake. Place in the fridge for about 1 hour to set.
4. Meanwhile, prepare the mixture for the filling. Place the cream cheese in a bowl with the icing sugar and cream together.
5. Add the double cream and vanilla extract and beat until smooth and creamy.
6. In a pan, mix the blueberries, sugar, water and lemon juice, and cook over low heat until the blueberries start to soften.
7. Remove from the heat and leave to cool slightly. Purée the blueberry mixture and pass through a sieve to remove any skin.
8. Swirl the purée into the cream mixture, then spoon into the jars. Top with some fresh blueberries.
9. Place in the fridge to set for a couple of hours or overnight. Just before serving, dust the tops of the cheesecakes with a little icing sugar.

Peter Pan

Wendy, John and Michael Darling lived in London with their parents and their nurse, Nana, a Newfoundland dog. One night Wendy awoke to find a strange boy in the nursery where they slept. Startled, Nana raced into the room and the boy flew out of the window, leaving his shadow behind.

The next night the boy returned for his shadow. 'Who are you?' asked Wendy. 'I'm Peter Pan.' Before long, Peter Pan was showing the children how to fly and telling them wonderful tales of a place called Neverland, where children never had to grow up. 'Take us there!' cried the children, and with that they flew out of the window with Tinkerbell the fairy. Soon they were flying over the sea, until they reached an island. 'This is where I live with the Lost Boys and Tinkerbell,' cried Peter Pan, as they swooped down to Neverland, the magical realm of fairies, mermaids and Native Americans.

For a while they were happy – Wendy took care of the Lost Boys, telling them stories and tucking them into bed each night. Peter and the boys played games and had wild adventures on the island. But not everything was perfect in Neverland. One day, while the children were exploring the lagoon, Peter yelled, 'Pirates!' The pirates were led by Captain Hook, Peter Pan's enemy. His one weakness was the crocodile who had eaten off his hand, and wanted more of him!

Wendy and the boys soon began to feel homesick and asked Peter if he would come home with them. But Peter said he could never live somewhere where grown-ups told him what to do. The next morning they were preparing to leave when Captain Hook's pirates captured them all, tied them up, and marched them to the pirate ship. Tinkerbell escaped and flew off to find Peter. A sword fight ensued and eventually the evil Hook fell into the water, to be swallowed up by the waiting crocodile.

Peter flew the children home to London, where their distraught parents hugged them and agreed to adopt all the Lost Boys – as well as Peter Pan. But Peter said he wanted to return to Neverland, so he would never have to grow up. And with that, he flew home.

Pirate Ship Cake

Sail away in your very own pirate ship, complete with sails made of cake lace.

- 1 x 20-cm (8-in) square cake (see page 15)
- 1 kg (2¼ lb) buttercream (see page 19)
- 500 g (1 lb 2 oz) fondant
- Brown and black food colouring pastes
- Brown and black petal dusts
- 100 g (3½ oz) cake lace kit
- 3 wooden skewers

ASSEMBLE THE CAKE

1 After baking and cooling, cut the cake layers in half so you have four 10 x 20-cm (4 x 8-in) cakes. Level and fill one of these with buttercream (see page 13), then taper all four sides to resemble the shape of a ship.

2 From the remaining cake, cut one layer into a 7.5 x 10-cm (3 x 4-in) rectangle and attach to the back of the ship with a layer of buttercream.

3 Now cut two rectangles of cake, each 4 x 10 cm (2 x 4 in). Layer one of these on the back of the cake, and the other on the front of the cake.

4 Cut another two rectangles measuring 2.5 x 10 cm (1 x 4 in) and layer onto the back and the front of the cake.

5 Carve the cake to soften the edges and create a more pointed hull.

6 Crumb coat the whole cake with buttercream.

7 Colour the fondant brown and roll out to a thickness of 5 mm (¼ in). Imprint with a woodgrain texture mat.

8 Cut out strips of fondant 2.5 cm (1 in) wide and of varying lengths. Paint these with brown and black coloured petal dusts to give the wood panels an aged look.

9 Arrange these strips of fondant horizontally on the sides of the cake to resemble planks of wood.

10 Cut out strips of fondant 10 cm (4 in) long and attach these to the steps on the front and back of the cake and the floor of the ship, until the whole cake is covered.

11 Use a toothpick to indent holes in the planks on each end.

MAKE THE SAILS

1 Make some cake lace paste according to the packet instructions. Colour it black using food colouring paste.

2 Spread the paste into the silicone lace mat and allow to set.

3 Peel away from the mat and cut three pieces of lace that are approximately 10 cm (4 in) wide: one 20 cm (8 in) in length and two 15 cm (6 in) in length.

4 Thread each one through a wooden skewer and then attach to the cake so that the middle sail is the tallest.

Peter Pan Hat Fortune Cookies

Why not add quotes from the story of Peter Pan to your fortune cookie paper strips?

MAKES 12–15

2 egg whites (60 ml/2 fl oz)
80 g (2¾ oz) sugar
60 g (2 oz) unsalted butter, melted and cooled
100 g (3½ oz) plain flour
¼ tsp salt
Green and red colouring pastes
Strips of paper with a fortune or a quote
20 g (¾ oz) gum paste
Small amount of royal icing

1. Preheat the oven to 180°C (350°F) and line a baking sheet with baking parchment.
2. Whisk the eggs whites on high speed with an electric mixer until they start to become white and foamy.
3. Add the sugar and continue to beat until soft peaks form.
4. Pour in the melted butter, flour, salt and green food colouring and mix well. The batter will look like a thin pancake batter.
5. Spoon a tablespoon of the mixture onto the prepared baking sheet, then use the back of the spoon to spread it to a circle 7.5 cm (3 in) wide.
6. Repeat this twice (cookies harden very quickly, so make only two or three at a time).
7. Bake for 5–6 minutes, until the edges start to turn golden brown.
8. Remove the cookies from the oven and lift up using a palette knife. Add a strip of paper with a fortune or quote, fold the cookie in half over the paper to make a semicircle, then rest the middle of the cookie across the rim of a glass and bend the edges down to fold the cookie inwards.
9. Place in a cupcake tin to cool so it retains its shape. Repeat with the remaining batter.
10. While the cookies are cooling, colour the gum paste red and use it to make 12 feathers, following the instructions on page 106. Attach the feathers to the cooled cookies using a dab of royal icing.

Before long, Peter Pan was showing the children how to fly and telling them wonderful tales of a place called Neverland, where children never had to grow up.

Tinkerbell Mini Cakes

If you don't have mini cake tins, you can bake this as a square cake and cut out mini cakes using a cookie cutter.

MAKES 12

1 quantity of 18-cm (7-in) round cake batter, used to make 12 mini cakes (see page 15)
500 g (1 lb 2 oz) buttercream (see page 19)
1.2 kg (2½ lb) fondant
Green and pink food colouring pastes
Dark green petal dust
2 tbsp royal icing
20 g (¾ oz) gum paste
40 g (1½ oz) cake lace kit or isomalt nibs
Edible glue (optional)

1. Preheat the oven to 170°C (340°F). Make the cake batter and fill twelve mini 5-cm (2-in) round cake tins two-thirds full. Bake for 20–25 minutes, until a skewer inserted into the centre comes out clean. Remove the cakes from the oven and leave to cool. Alternatively, bake a 23-cm (9-in) square cake (see page 15) and use a 5-cm (2-in) cookie cutter to cut 12 circles.

2. When cool, remove from the tins and use a serrated knife to slice off the tops to level the cakes. Slice the cakes in half, fill with buttercream in the middle, and sandwich together. Crumb coat the cakes all over (see page 9).

3. Colour the fondant light green and roll out to a thickness of 3 mm (⅛ in). Completely cover each cake with the fondant (see page 11).

4. Use dark green petal dust to darken the base of the cakes.

5. Colour the royal icing green and spoon into a piping bag fitted with a round tip. Pipe swirling vines around the base of the cakes.

6. Colour the gum paste pink and roll out. Use cutters to cut out tiny blossoms and attach to the piped vines.

7. Either make up the cake lace according to the packet instructions or melt the isomalt nibs and pour into a butterfly lace mould. Leave to set.

8. Once it has set, remove the butterflies from the mould and position them on the top of the cakes, attaching them with royal icing or edible glue.

Soon they were flying over the sea, until they reached an island. 'This is where I live with the Lost Boys and Tinkerbell,' cried Peter Pan.

A sword fight ensued and eventually the evil Hook fell into the water, to be swallowed up by the waiting crocodile.

Captain Hook Cupcakes

Make the little hooks for these cupcakes in advance, to give them plenty of time to set.

MAKES 12

200 g (7 oz) white gum paste
Grey and red food colouring pastes
Edible silver paint
Gold lustre dust
12 chocolate cupcakes (see page 18)
500 g (1 lb 2 oz) buttercream (see page 19)

MAKE THE HOOKS

1 To make the hooks, colour approximately 115 g (4 oz) of the gum paste grey and roll it into 12 sausage shapes. Take one sausage and taper at one end to make a pointy edge. Curve around into a hook shape and place on a foam drying tray to set. Repeat to make 12 hooks and then paint each one with edible silver paint.

2 Thinly roll out the remaining white gum paste and cut it into 12 rectangles, each 5 x 12.5 cm (2 x 5 in).

3 Frill using a ball tool on a foam pad. Place the ball tool half on the gum paste and half on the foam pad and apply pressure as you move the ball tool along the length of the paste. You may need to repeat the action a few times to achieve a frilly effect. Loop the frills into circles and allow to set.

4 Once they have set, dust some gold lustre dust onto the edges of the frills.

ASSEMBLE THE CUPCAKES

1 While they are setting, bake the cupcakes and allow to cool fully.

2 Colour the buttercream red using red food colouring paste and then spoon into a piping bag fitted with a large round tip. Pipe swirls on top of each cupcake, then insert the frills into the tops. Push the hooks into the middle of the cupcakes.

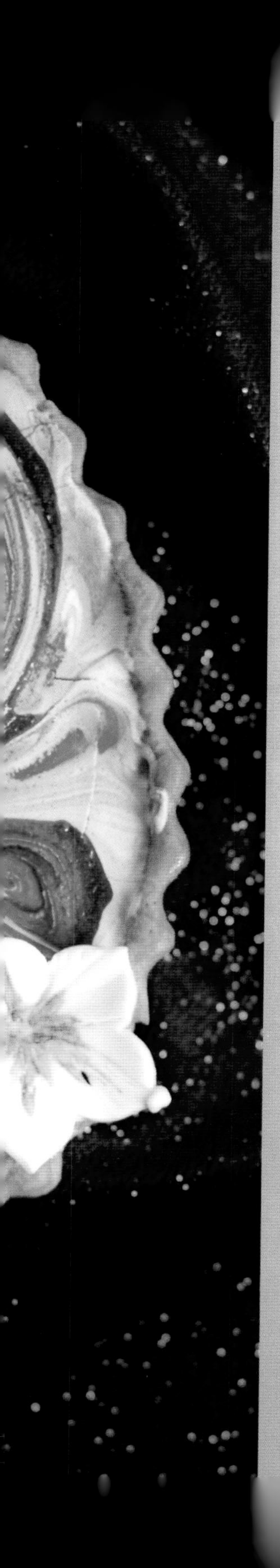

Thumbelina

There was once a kind woman who longed for a baby. 'How I would love to have a baby girl, however tiny!' she would cry. One day a beautiful fairy heard her wish and gave her a tiny plant in a flowerpot. The woman softly kissed the petals of the flower and as if by magic, the flower opened. Inside sat a tiny girl, no bigger than a thumb.

The woman loved her and called her Thumbelina. She had a walnut shell for a bed and a rose petal for a blanket. Every day she played in a tulip petal boat and sailed around her little pond. But an ugly toad soon fell in love with the tiny girl and, while she was sleeping one night, he carried her off to his lily pad. Thumbelina was very unhappy and all she could do was cry her eyes out. But two little minnows felt sorry for her and nibbled away at the lily pad stem until it broke and floated away. Thumbelina was free from the ugly toad!

But other dangers lay ahead. A large beetle snatched her away and took her to his home at the top of a tree. But he soon felt sorry for her and set her free. Thumbelina was all alone and had to survive by drinking dew and eating pollen. She met many creatures on her way until finally she came to the house of a little field mouse. He invited her in and offered her food and shelter. For her keep Thumbelina did the housework and told the mouse stories.

One day she came across a wounded swallow. It broke her heart to see him, so every day she went to nurse the swallow and tenderly gave him food. In the meantime, the swallow told Thumbelina how he had been wounded by a thorn and unable to fly with his companions to a warmer climate. As the swallow's leg became stronger, Thumbelina realised that he would soon fly away and leave her.

'Take me with you!' she cried. She climbed onto the swallow's wings and the pair soared into the sky until they reached a beautiful land of flowers. The swallow gently laid Thumbelina on a blossom, where she met a tiny, white-winged fairy: the King of the Flower Fairies. They fell in love instantly and the king asked her to marry him. As soon as Thumbelina said 'Yes!' she sprouted tiny white wings. She was now the Flower Queen.

Lily Pad Tart

PASTRY
400 g (14 oz) plain flour, plus extra for dusting
100 g (3½ oz) icing sugar
Pinch of salt
200 g (7 oz) unsalted butter, cold and diced
2 egg yolks
1–2 tbsp cold milk

CRÈME PÂTISSIÈRE
475 ml (16 fl oz) milk
1 tsp vanilla extract
5 egg yolks
100 g (3½ oz) sugar
2 tbsp plain flour
2 tbsp cornflour
Blue food colouring paste

DECORATION
40 g (1½ oz) green gum paste
Green petal dust
Chocolate Truffle Birds (see page 146)
Sugar Flowers (see page 148)

You could also make this tart in smaller individual tart tins.

MAKE THE PASTRY BASE

1 Sift the flour, icing sugar and salt into a bowl. Add the diced butter and cut in together until the mixture resembles sand.

2 Make a well in the centre, then add the egg yolks and mix until the mixture starts to come together. Add some milk, a tablespoon at a time, to form a dough.

3 Turn out onto a floured surface and knead for 2 minutes, then place in the fridge to chill for 20 minutes.

4 While the dough is chilling, preheat the oven to 180°C (350°F). You will need a 20-cm (8-in) loose-bottomed flan tin.

5 Roll out the dough on a floured work surface to a thickness of approximately 5 mm (¼ in), making sure it is bigger than the tin.

6 Place the rolled dough into the tin, making sure you push it into the corners, then prick with a fork and place a piece of baking parchment over the dough. Fill with baking beans and bake for approximately 15 minutes until light golden brown. Remove the baking beans and parchment, then bake for a further 10 minutes.

MAKE THE CRÈME PÂTISSIÈRE

1 Place the milk and vanilla into a large saucepan and warm over low heat.

2 Place the egg yolks and sugar in a bowl and whisk until pale and creamy. Then add the flour and cornflour and continue to whisk until fully incorporated.

3 Add the warm milk mixture to the eggs in a slow, steady stream, while whisking slowly, then return the mixture to the pan.

4 Cook on low heat, stirring continuously, until the mixture thickens, then remove from the heat and place a piece of cling film directly on the surface to avoid a film forming as it cools.

5 Once it has cooled slightly, add blue food colouring and mix to form a pale blue colour, then add some more blue food colouring and half-mix to create a marbled effect. Pour into the prepared pastry base and leave to cool fully.

MAKE THE LILY PADS

1 Thinly roll out green coloured gum paste and cut two circles, one large, one small. Cut a triangular wedge out of each circle and press the lily pads into a leaf veiner.

2 Place them on a foam drying tray and put scrunched up pieces of cling film under the lily pads to give them a rippled look. Leave to set in position.

3 Once fully dry, dust with green petal dust and place on the tart. Decorate the tart with Chocolate Truffle Birds and Sugar Flowers (see pages 146 and 148).

Mini Walnut Cakes

Imagine being so tiny that your bed is a walnut! These tiny little cakes would be perfect for Thumbelina.

MAKES 6–8

175 g (6 oz) unsalted butter
175 g (6 oz) light brown sugar
175 g (6 oz) self-raising flour
3 eggs
70 g (2½ oz) chopped walnuts, plus 6–8 walnut halves, to decorate
500 g (1 lb 2 oz) buttercream (see page 19)

1. Preheat the oven to 160°C (325°F) and line 6–8 mini 5-cm (2-in) round cake tins with baking parchment.
2. Cream together the butter and sugar for a few minutes until pale and creamy.
3. Sift the flour into a separate bowl.
4. Add the eggs to the butter mixture, one at a time, along with a spoonful of flour to prevent the mixture curdling.
5. Once all the eggs are mixed in, fold in the remaining flour and add the chopped walnuts.
6. Fill the cake tins two-thirds full and bake for 20–22 minutes. Remove from the oven and leave to cool.
7. Remove from the cake tins and, using a serrated knife, slice off the tops to level the cakes.
8. Split the cakes in half, layer with buttercream in the middle and sandwich together.
9. Fit a piping bag with a small star tip and fill with the remaining buttercream. Add a swirl of buttercream to the top of the cakes and complete by adding a walnut half.

The woman loved her and called her Thumbelina. She had a walnut shell for a bed and a rose petal for a blanket.

Chocolate Truffle Birds

Choose dark or white chocolate for these little birds – or make a selection of both!

MAKES 20–25

- 200 g (7 oz) dark or white chocolate, broken into pieces
- 200 ml (7 fl oz) double cream, or 100 ml (3½ fl oz) if using white chocolate
- 25 g (1 oz) unsalted butter
- Bird-shaped chocolate moulds
- Cocoa powder, for dusting, or crushed freeze-dried raspberries, for sprinkling

1. Place a heat-proof bowl over a pan of simmering water. Add the chocolate and cream to the bowl and allow to melt. Do not let the water touch the bowl.
2. Remove from the heat, add the butter and stir well.
3. Pour into a mixing bowl and whisk for a few minutes, until the mixture cools down.
4. Spoon the mixture into bird moulds and place in the fridge to set.
5. Once set, remove the chocolate birds from the moulds and finish by dusting with cocoa powder or sprinkling with crushed freeze-dried raspberries.

One day Thumbelina came across a wounded swallow. It broke her heart to see him, so every day she went to nurse the swallow and tenderly gave him food.

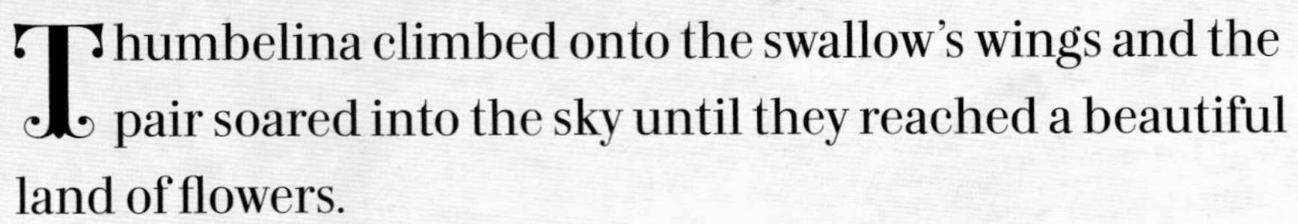

Thumbelina climbed onto the swallow's wings and the pair soared into the sky until they reached a beautiful land of flowers.

Sugar Flowers

You will need a variety of flower cutters to make these – blossoms, petunias and small petals.

Gum paste
Petal dusts
Food colouring pastes
Rejuvenator spirit
Edible glue

MAKE THE BLOSSOMS AND PETUNIAS

1. Roll out some gum paste to a thickness of approximately 1–2 mm (1⁄16 in). Use your cutters to cut small and large blossom and petunia flower shapes from the gum paste.
2. Place the petals in a veiner and push down to create detailed petals.
3. Place in a foam drying tray to set for 1–2 hours.
4. Once dry, dust the edges with petal dust. You can also mix some paste colours with 1–2 drops of rejuvenator spirit and use this to paint veined details in the flowers.

MAKE THE DAHLIAS

1. To make a dahlia flower, cut out approximately 16–20 small petal shapes. Soften with a ball tool and pinch the ends together to cup each petal.
2. Arrange 10–12 of these petals in a circle and attach in the middle using edible glue.
3. Then arrange another 6–8 petals in a circle above the first layer and attach together using edible glue. Place a ball of gum paste in the middle and indent using a round piping tip.

Alice in Wonderland

A young girl called Alice sat on a riverbank, bored and drowsy in the warm sunshine. Suddenly, she spied a talking white rabbit hurrying past, looking at a pocket watch and muttering, 'I'm late!' He disappeared down a rabbit hole, Alice tumbled in after him, and found herself in a room with many doors of different sizes. On a table, Alice found a tiny gold key and a green bottle that said 'Drink Me'. She drank the potion and soon began to shrink, until she was no bigger than a doll. Excitedly, she ran through one of the doors and found herself in a wonderful garden. She soon tired of being so small and shouted, 'I want to be big again!' Seeing the White Rabbit, she followed him to a little cottage, where she found a piece of cake, labelled 'Eat Me'. She did just that, and suddenly she felt herself growing until she was an enormous size. She began to shrink again. She wandered through the garden and came across a caterpillar sitting on a mushroom. He offered her a piece of the mushroom and she started to grow.

Wandering through the strange garden, she came across a smiling Cheshire Cat in a tree, who directed her toward the Mad Hatter. The Mad Hatter was a curious fellow, who said she could come to his tea party as long as she answered his riddles. She became increasingly frustrated with the Mad Hatter and continued her walk. She soon found herself in the middle of a field where the Queen of Hearts was playing croquet. All the guards and gardeners were shaped like playing cards and the gardeners were painting red the white roses that they had planted by mistake. 'I hate white roses,' shrieked the queen. 'Off with their heads!' When the queen saw Alice she ordered her to play croquet – with a flamingo and a hedgehog. Suddenly, a trumpet sounded and everyone rushed to the courtroom. Alice found that it was she who was on trial, accused of stealing the queen's tarts. Once again the queen shouted, 'Off with her head!'

Just then, Alice felt someone touch her shoulder and heard a voice saying, 'Wake up.' It was her sister, and she realised she had been dreaming. As she stretched, Alice was certain she saw a little white rabbit scurrying behind a tree...

Mad Hatter's Teapot Cake

For this project you will need a 12.5-cm (5-in) ball cake tin.

700 g (1½ lb) grey fondant
3 toothpicks
1 quantity of 12.5-cm (5-in) round cake batter (see page 15)
400 g (14 oz) buttercream (see page 19)
Edible glue
Green, pink and orange gum pastes

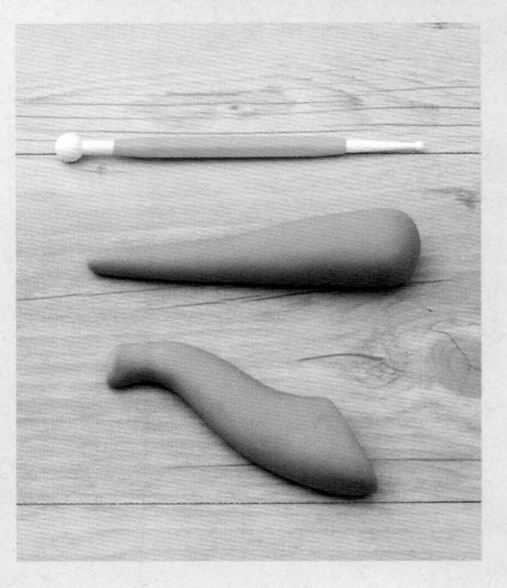

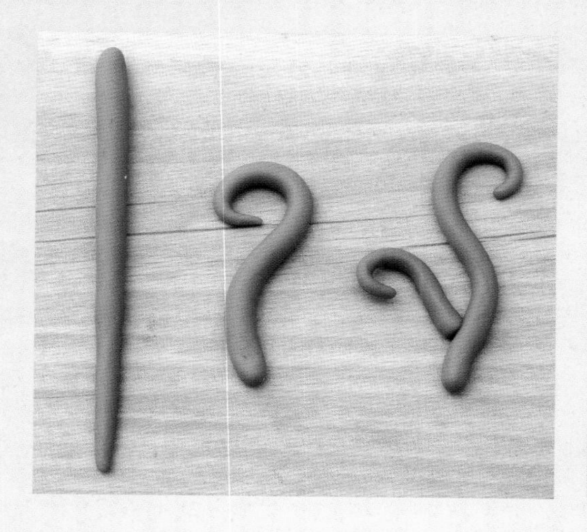

1 Make the teapot spout and handle first so they have sufficient time to dry. Take approximately 80 g (2¾ oz) of grey fondant and shape it into a long spout shape, use a ball tool to indent the opening, then gently curve into shape. Insert a toothpick in the base of the spout and set aside on a foam drying tray.

2 Take 50 g (1¾ oz) of grey fondant for the handle. Roll it into a long sausage shape and taper the ends so they are thinner than the rest of the handle.

3 Curve the ends into swirls and shape the handle into an 'S' shape. Insert two toothpicks into the handle where it will meet the teapot and set aside on a foam drying tray.

4 Preheat the oven to 160°C (325°F). Make up the cake batter and pour into the 12.5-cm (5-in) ball cake tins. Bake for 20–25 minutes.

5 Once the cakes have been baked, use a serrated knife to slice off the domed tops. Spread some buttercream over one of the halves. Sandwich the two halves together and crumb coat the whole cake with the remaining buttercream (see page 9). Place in the fridge to set for 20 minutes.

6 Roll out 500 g (1 lb 2 oz) of the grey fondant and cover the ball cake completely, trimming off any excess (see page 12).

7 Roll out the remaining grey fondant to a thickness of 3 mm (⅛ in) and use a large circle cutter 9 cm (3½ in) in diameter to cut out a lid for the teapot. Attach using edible glue.

8 Roll a small ball of grey fondant from the offcuts and attach it to the top of the lid using edible glue.

9 Attach the spout and handle by inserting the toothpicks into the side of the cake and securing with royal icing.

10 Roll some green coloured gum paste into long thin sausages and attach them to the cake in swirl patterns using edible glue.

11 Roll out pink and orange coloured gum paste to a thickness of 1–2 mm (1/16 in) and cut out different-sized blossoms.

12 Using a dab of edible glue, attach a smaller blossom in the middle of a larger blossom, then complete by attaching a tiny ball of green fondant in the middle of the flower. Place these on a foam drying tray to dry, then attach to the cake using edible glue.

Pocket Watch Cupcakes

Make the pocket watches in advance so there is enough drying time before you place them on the cupcakes.

MAKES 12

POCKET WATCHES

150 g (5¼ oz) gum paste
Gold and black food colouring pastes
Edible glue
Toothpick
Metallic lustre
Small amount of black royal icing

CUPCAKES

12 chocolate cupcakes (see page 18)
500 g (1 lb 2 oz) buttercream (see page 19)

MAKE THE POCKET WATCHES

1 Colour 90 g (3 oz) of the gum paste gold and then roll out to a thickness of around 4–5 mm (¼ in).

2 Use a round cutter to cut out 12 circles the same diameter as your cupcakes and place to one side.

3 Roll out white gum paste to a thickness of 3 mm (⅛ in).

4 Cut out 12 circles just smaller than the gold circles, and place them on top of the gold circles. Attach using edible glue.

5 Take a small ball of gold gum paste and place it at the top of the gold circle. Make tiny indents using a toothpick.

6 Roll a small sausage from gold gum paste and place this on top of the ball. Leave to dry for 2 hours.

7 Once dry, dust or paint with metallic lustre.

8 Write the clock numbers using black royal icing using a piping bag fitted with a size 0 tip. Finally pipe on the watch hands.

MAKE THE CUPCAKES

1 Prepare and bake the cupcakes (see page 18). Remove from the oven and leave to cool in the cupcake tin for 10 minutes, then leave to cool completely on a wire cooling rack.

2 Fit a piping bag with a star-shaped tip, fill with the prepared buttercream and pipe swirls on top of each cupcake.

3 Place the prepared pocket watches on top of the buttercream swirls.

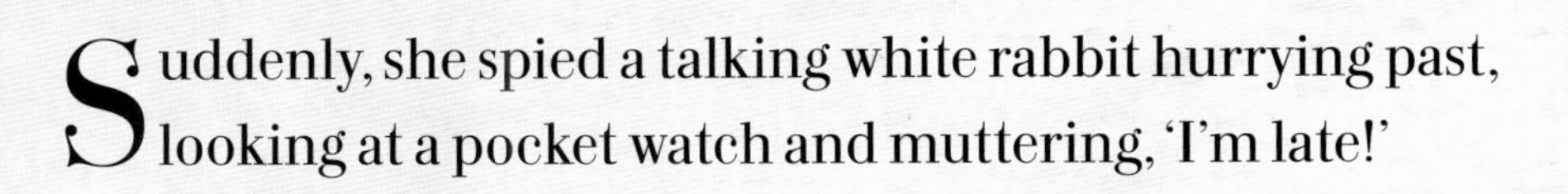

Suddenly, she spied a talking white rabbit hurrying past, looking at a pocket watch and muttering, 'I'm late!'

Marshmallow White Rabbits

You can either make a large tray of marshmallow and cut out shapes using a rabbit-shaped cutter, or pour into rabbit-shaped chocolate moulds.

MAKES 20–30

- 250 ml (8½ fl oz) water
- 4 tbsp unflavoured powdered gelatine
- 400 g (14 oz) sugar, plus extra for dusting
- 2 tbsp golden syrup
- 2 egg whites (60 ml/2 fl oz)
- 2 tsp vanilla extract
- 100 g (3½ oz) icing sugar, for dusting

1. Place half of the water in a bowl and sprinkle the gelatine over the surface. Set aside for 10 minutes to allow it to bloom, then heat it up in the microwave for approximately 10 seconds until the gelatine has dissolved completely.
2. Meanwhile, in a small saucepan, mix together the sugar, golden syrup and remaining water and heat on medium to high heat. Place a sugar thermometer in the pan to accurately check the temperature. Once the sugar has dissolved completely, reduce the heat to low. The temperature of the syrup will continue to rise, bring it up to 125°C (257°F).
3. While the sugar is heating, place the egg whites into the bowl of a stand mixer fitted with a whisk attachment. As soon as the sugar syrup reaches the right temperature, start mixing the egg whites until they reach the soft peak stage.
4. Add the gelatine mixture to the sugar syrup and stir well. Add the vanilla extract.
5. Carefully pour the syrup mixture onto the egg whites in a thin stream, and continue to whisk for approximately 10 minutes until the egg whites are very stiff.
6. Dust either the rabbit-shaped chocolate moulds or a 25-cm (10-in) cake tin with icing sugar and pour the mixture in. Use a wet palette knife to flatten the top, then allow to set for 2–3 hours.
7. Dust your work surface with icing sugar and turn out the marshmallow from the moulds or cake tin. If you have prepared the marshmallow in a cake tin, use the rabbit cutter to make rabbit shapes.
8. Finish by coating the rabbits in icing sugar.

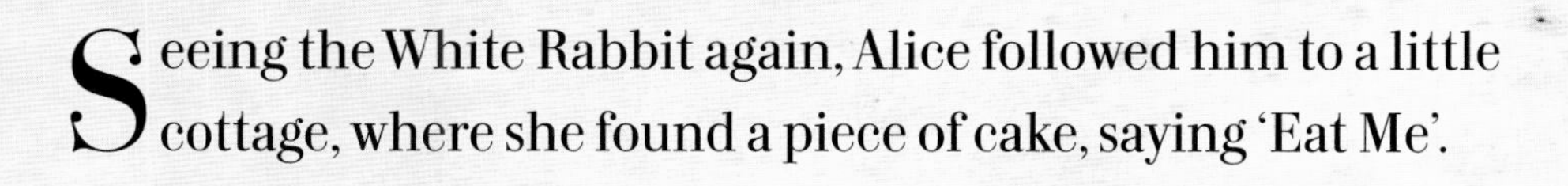

Seeing the White Rabbit again, Alice followed him to a little cottage, where she found a piece of cake, saying 'Eat Me'.

Alice soon found herself in the middle of a field where the Queen of Hearts was playing croquet. All the guards and gardeners were shaped like playing cards.

Queen of Hearts Tarts

Make sure no one steals these delicious heart-shaped tarts – or it's off with their head!

MAKES 12–15

200 g (7 oz) plain flour, plus extra for dusting
50 g (1¾ oz) icing sugar, plus extra for dusting
Pinch of salt
100 g (3½ oz) unsalted butter, cold and diced
1 egg yolk
Splash of cold milk
100 g (3½ oz) raspberry or strawberry conserve

1. Sift the flour, sugar and salt into a bowl. Add in the diced butter and cut in together until the mixture resembles sand.
2. Make a well in the centre, then add the egg yolk and mix until it starts to come together. Add some milk, a tablespoon at a time, to form a dough.
3. Turn out onto a floured work surface and knead for 2 minutes, then place in the fridge to chill for 20 minutes.
4. Flour the work surface once again and roll out the dough to a thickness of approximately 5 mm (¼ in).
5. Use a large heart-shaped cutter to cut out hearts and place them on a baking sheet lined with baking parchment. Use a smaller heart-shaped cutter to cut windows out of half of the dough hearts. It is important to do this while they are on the baking sheet, since moving them can distort their shape. Prick the dough hearts a few times using a fork, then chill in the fridge for 30 minutes before baking.
6. Preheat the oven to 180°C (350°F).
7. Spread a teaspoon of conserve onto each of the whole heart shapes.
8. Bake for approximately 15 minutes, until golden brown.
9. Remove from the oven and leave to cool slightly, then place the cut-out hearts on top of the preserve-covered hearts and leave to cool fully.
10. Finish with a light dusting of icing sugar.

Beauty and the Beast

Once upon a time in a far-off country, there lived a rich merchant and his daughter Beauty, along with his five other daughters and six sons. But the merchant fell on hard times and lost all his wealth and the family fell into great poverty. One day, the father received word that one of his ships had been found and they were no longer poor. He set off to go to the ship, but got lost in a dark forest. Soon he stumbled upon a beautiful castle. Being tired and hungry, he wandered into the house, ate the food that was laid out and explored the vast halls. On leaving the castle he saw a beautiful rose bush and decided to pluck a rose for his youngest and most precious daughter, Beauty. Suddenly, a frightful beast, the owner of the castle, appeared and discovered the terrified merchant. The Beast was furious with the merchant for stealing the rose but told the merchant he would let him go if he promised to come back with his daughter. With a sad heart the merchant returned home. Beauty, on hearing of the Beast's request, insisted on going to the castle to spare her father's life. There she was treated with kindness and showered with gifts and luxuries. Although she was initially scared of the hideous Beast, as time went by she became less afraid, and slowly she began to like him. However, when the Beast asked for her hand in marriage, she could not accept. She longed to see her father so the Beast showed her a magic mirror, in which she saw the image of her father, ill and alone. She begged to be released and with great sadness the Beast let her go, begging her to return to him after seven days. Beauty returned home and tended to her father and soon forgot all about the Beast. But one night she had a terrible nightmare, in which she saw the Beast overcome with sadness and slowly dying, crying, 'Beauty, please come back!' She ran to the castle and found the Beast lying on the floor. She threw her arms around him, crying, 'I will never leave you!' All of a sudden the Beast turned into a handsome prince, who told Beauty that he had been put under a spell that would only be broken when he found his true love and made her love him back.

Rose Garden Cake

Make the roses and leaves for this pretty cake in advance so they are fully set by the time you need to use them.

1 x 18-cm (7-in) round cake (see page 15)
650 g (1½ lb) buttercream (see page 19)
1 kg (2¼ lb) white fondant
3 cake dowels
Royal icing or edible glue
Floral wire or toothpick
Green florists' tape
Bell jar

ROSES AND LEAVES
150 g (5¼ oz) red gum paste
50 g (1¾ oz) green gum paste
Edible glue
Petal dusts

MAKE THE ROSES

1 Knead the red gum paste and roll an olive-sized piece of paste into a cone shape and set aside.

2 Roll out some more gum paste to a thickness of approximately 3 mm (⅛ in).

3 Using a rose petal cutter, cut between four and 16 petals, depending on how large you want the rose to be.

4 Wrap the first rose petal around the cone to make a spiral shape to form the centre of the rose and attach with edible glue.

5 Take three petals for the next layer and soften the edges using a ball tool, then curl the edges of the rose petals with a toothpick to create a more natural look.

6 Wrap each petal around the cone, making sure to overlap as you place the next petal. Stop here if you want to form a rosebud.

7 Continue placing petals, going up in odd numbers. Place five petals for the next layer, seven for the next, and so on.

8 Pinch around the base of the rose to firmly attach the petals, then use a palette knife to cut off any excess gum paste at the base. Repeat to make six roses.

9 Roll out some green gum paste to a thickness of 3 mm (⅛ in) and use a calyx cutter to cut a calyx for each rose. Attach to the base of the rose using water or edible glue.

MAKE THE LEAVES

1. Roll out the green gum paste to a thickness of 2 mm (1/16 in). Using a leaf cutter, cut out 10 leaves. If you wish, you can also lightly score the leaves to create veins.
2. Place on a foam drying tray at different angles to dry the leaves in a variety of positions.
3. Once dry, use petal dusts to highlight the leaves and give them extra dimension.

ASSEMBLE THE CAKE

1. Level the 18-cm (7-in) cake layers, fill with buttercream, and crumb coat (see pages 9 and 13).
2. Roll out about three-quarters of the white fondant and use to cover the cake, smoothing out any creases using cake smoothers (see page 11).
3. Measure the circumference of the cake at the top and split into five equal segments. Mark the five points using a toothpick.

MAKE THE SWAGS

1. Roll out the remaining white fondant to a thickness of 3 mm (⅛ in) and cut five rectangles that are approximately 5–7.5 cm (2–3 in) longer than the distance between the points, and approximately 7.5–10 cm (3–4 in) wide.
2. Place three wooden or plastic dowels horizontally on your work surface, 2.5 cm (1 in) apart.
3. Place a rectangle of fondant across the top of the dowels, then shape the fondant around the dowels so that the folds are visible.
4. Push the dowels together so that the fondant gathers and forms visible creases.
5. Carefully remove the dowels and pinch the ends together to join them.
6. Place royal icing or edible glue on the edge of the cake in a swag shape, starting at one of the five marked points, curving down and then up to meet the next marked point. Attach the fondant to the cake to form a swag.
7. Repeat this for the remaining four pieces so you have a swag pattern all the way around the cake.

POSITION THE ROSES AND LEAVES

1. Position the roses and leaves where the swags meet each other to hide the joins and secure with edible glue.
2. For the remaining rose, push a floral wire or toothpick in at the base and wrap with green florists' tape.
3. Position this rose in the centre of the cake, with some fallen petals around it.
4. Complete by covering the rose with a bell jar.

Rose Macarons

These delicate macarons are easy to make – try piping in heart shapes, rather than the traditional round shape.

MAKES 15

- 70 g (2½ oz) ground almonds
- 100 g (3½ oz) icing sugar
- 2 large egg whites (approximately 60 ml/2 fl oz)
- ¼ tsp cream of tartar (optional)
- 50 g (1¾ oz) caster sugar
- Pink food colouring paste or gel
- Crystallised rose petals (optional)
- 300 g (10½ oz) buttercream or chocolate ganache (see pages 19 and 20)

1. Place the ground almonds and icing sugar in the bowl of a food processor and process until finely ground. Sift this into another bowl, and discard anything left in the sieve. Set to one side.
2. Whisk the egg whites until they reach the soft peak stage, then add the cream of tartar (this is optional but it can help to stabilise the egg).
3. Add the caster sugar, a tablespoon at a time, and pink food colouring and continue to whisk until you reach the stiff peak stage.
4. Add the almond/sugar mixture slowly in three batches, folding it in after each addition using a spatula in a cut-and-fold action, taking care not to overwork the mixture. The mixture should appear thick and ribbon-like.
5. Fit a piping bag with a round tip, fill with the mixture and pipe the macarons onto a baking sheet lined with baking parchment. Create heart shapes by piping in a 'V' shape.
6. Tap the baking sheet firmly on your work surface a few times and allow to rest for at least 30–40 minutes until a film has formed. Check this by lightly touching the surface of a macaron – it should not be wet or come off onto your finger. If it is still wet, allow to rest a little longer. If you wish, sprinkle the tops of the macarons with crystallised rose petals before resting. Preheat the oven to 150°C (300°F).
7. Bake the macarons for 13–15 minutes. They should rise and form little 'feet' at the base and come away from the baking parchment easily. Remove from the oven and leave to cool, then remove from the baking sheet.
8. Pipe buttercream or chocolate ganache between the cooled shells and sandwich together.

On leaving the castle, the merchant saw a beautiful rose bush and decided to pluck a rose for his youngest and most precious daughter, Beauty.

Rose in a Jar Cake

You will need 12 mini cake tins to make these pretty layered cakes, as well as eight small, wide-mouthed jars.

MAKES 8

1 quantity of 15-cm (6-in) round cake batter (see page 15), flavoured with 1 tsp rose extract
Pink food colouring paste
650 g (1½ lb) buttercream (see page 19)

1. Preheat the oven to 160°C (325°F) and line 12 mini cake tins, 5 cm (2 in) in diameter, with baking parchment.
2. Mix the cake batter and colour it very pale pink using a little pink food colouring paste. Put one-third of the cake batter into four of the prepared mini cake tins.
3. Colour the remaining cake batter with more food colouring to make a slightly darker pink. Fill four of the mini cake tins with half of this batter.
4. Colour the last portion of cake batter to make the darkest shade of pink and fill the remaining mini cake tins with this batter.
5. Bake for 20–25 minutes, or until a skewer inserted into the centre comes out clean.
6. Once the cakes have cooled, remove them from the cake tins and, using a serrated knife, slice off the domed tops.
7. Slice the cakes in half horizontally, then start to assemble.
8. Place the darkest pink cake into the bottom of a jar.
9. Using a piping bag fitted with a star tip, pipe a swirl of buttercream on top of the cake – start by piping in the middle, then swirl the buttercream outward, finishing on the edge of the cake.
10. Place a medium-pink layer of cake on top of the buttercream and repeat this again, with the palest pink layer of cake at the very top, to give an ombre effect. Pipe a buttercream rose on the last layer of cake to finish.

The Beast was furious with the merchant for stealing the rose but told the merchant he would let him go if he promised to come back with his daughter.

Beauty longed to see her father so the Beast showed her a magic mirror, in which she saw the image of her father.

Mirror Cookies

Edible metallic paint will make these cute mirror cookies look even more realistic!

MAKES 15

1 quantity of cookie dough (see page 18)

ROYAL ICING

3 tbsp (30 g) powdered egg white
110 ml (3¾ fl oz) warm water
¼ tsp cream of tartar
600 g (1 lb 5 oz) icing sugar
Gold and silver food colouring pastes
Edible metallic paint (optional)

1 Chill the cookie dough for 15 minutes, then roll out on a floured surface to 5 mm (¼ in) thick.

2 Using a mirror-shaped cookie cutter, cut out the shapes and place on a baking sheet lined with baking parchment. Chill for 30 minutes – this will ensure the cookies won't spread and will stay flat to allow for decorating. Preheat the oven to 180°C (350°F).

3 Bake for 7–8 minutes, until they stop looking wet on the surface. They will still be soft at this stage but will continue to harden when removed from the oven. Leave to cool completely before decorating.

4 To make the royal icing, mix the powdered egg white with the water and cream of tartar until just incorporated. Add the sugar and mix with an electric hand mixer on low speed for 5 minutes.

5 Colour half of the royal icing gold. Fit a piping bag with a small round tip, fill with the gold royal icing and pipe an outline around the edge of the cookies. Pipe another outline for the inner edge of the mirror frame.

6 Set 2 tablespoons of the gold royal icing aside for the decoration and add a few drops of water to the remainder. Mix until you get a slightly thinner consistency (see page 12). Fill a piping bag or a squeezy bottle and flood the cookies up to the outlines.

7 Colour the remaining royal icing silver and use to fill in the inside of the mirror.

8 After the icing has completely set, decorate the handle and frame of the mirror using the reserved gold royal icing. Pipe swirls and dots to make the mirror more ornate.

9 Allow to set for 24 hours. Paint the dried cookies with edible metallic paint, if desired.

Aladdin

In a city in China long ago, there lived a poor widow and her only son, Aladdin. Aladdin was an idle boy, who always avoided hard work, much to his mother's despair. One day, while in the bazaar, Aladdin met Abanazar, a wicked sorcerer, who persuaded Aladdin to help him find something in return for his own carpet shop. He took him to a cave, gave him a magic ring for protection, and told him to go and find a lamp.

But when Aladdin returned to the cave's entrance with the lamp, Abanazar tried to trick him by telling him to pass up the lamp. Sensing danger, Aladdin refused so Abanazar sealed the cave, leaving Aladdin trapped inside. In despair, Aladdin rubbed his hands and inadvertently rubbed the magic ring. All at once a genie appeared and helped Aladdin escape.

When he arrived home he showed his mother the lamp. Unimpressed by the rusty and battered lamp, she told him to polish it. In a flash, another genie appeared like a wreath of smoke, coming out of the mouth of the lamp.

'What is your wish, Oh Master?' the genie asked. Aladdin and his mother asked for food and riches and for a while they were happy. But before long Aladdin began to feel that his life was not complete. He had fallen madly in love with the beautiful Princess Jasmine, the sultan's daughter. With the help of the genie, the sultan agreed to the marriage and for a while Aladdin and Jasmine lived happily in a magnificent palace that the genie had built for them.

But it is not a happy ending just yet. Abanazar, furious to hear of Aladdin's good fortune, returned with an evil plot to trick Jasmine. Unaware of the lamp's importance, she gave Abanazar the lamp in exchange for an ordinary, but more beautiful one. As soon as the sorcerer had the magic lamp he banished Jasmine and her palace to a hidden desert, never to be seen again.

Aladdin soon realised that Abanazar was behind this wicked plot. By good fortune, he had kept the magic ring. The genie of the ring transported Aladdin across the desert to be reunited with his wife and the magic lamp. He rubbed it and again the genie appeared.

'What is your wish, Oh Master?'

'Take us home!' Aladdin replied. 'Oh wonderful genie, take us home!' And they lived in great happiness until the day they died.

Pillow Cake

This easy but impressive cake is just a square cake that has had its sides tapered to resemble a pillow.

- 1 x 15-cm (6-in) square cake (see page 15)
- 650 g (1½ lb) buttercream (see page 19)
- 1 kg (2¼ lb) fondant
- Purple and gold food colouring pastes
- Edible glue
- Edible gold metallic paint
- 20 g (¾ oz) royal icing

1. After baking and cooling, level and stack the cake layers with buttercream (see page 13).
2. Make a pillow shape by carving the edges of the cake at an angle so that they taper inward, toward the middle of the cake. Remove any sharp edges by trimming them.
3. Turn the cake over and repeat this on the other side. Crumb coat the whole cake with buttercream (see page 9).
4. Colour 900 g (2 lb) of the fondant purple and roll it out to a thickness of 3 mm (⅛ in). Use it to cover the top half of the cake and trim where it meets the middle of the pillow.
5. Turn the cake over and repeat, so that the seam of fondant meets around the middle of the cake.
6. Colour the remaining fondant gold and then roll out into two long, thin sausages. Twist them together to resemble rope. Attach around the middle of the cake using edible glue.
7. Use a sugar gun fitted with a mesh disc to squeeze out gold fondant strands for the tassels (or shape them by hand). Cut off 7.5-cm (3-in) long tassels and attach to the corners of the cake with edible glue.
8. Roll four small balls of fondant and attach to the top of the tassels with edible glue.
9. Allow to set, then paint the rope and tassels with edible gold metallic paint.
10. Colour the royal icing with gold food colouring paste, then place in a piping bag fitted with a round tip. Use to pipe swirls and paisley designs on the pillow.
11. Allow the royal icing to dry, then paint with edible gold paint.

Magic Carpet Cookies

Make these magic carpet cookies as ornate as you wish by piping with gold royal icing.

MAKES 10–12

- 1 quantity of cookie dough (see page 18)
- 300 g (10½ oz) royal icing
- Blue, red and gold food colouring pastes
- Edible gold paint

1. Make the cookie dough and then chill in the fridge for 30 minutes, before rolling out onto a floured surface to a thickness of 5 mm (¼ in).
2. Cut out cookie shapes. Use a rectangular-shaped cookie cutter or cut freehand using the template on page 186 as a guide. Place them on a baking sheet lined with baking parchment. Chill for 30 minutes before baking – this will ensure the cookies don't spread and will stay flat to allow for decorating. Preheat the oven to 180°C (350°F).
3. Bake for 7–8 minutes, until they stop looking wet on the surface. They will still be soft at this stage, but do not overbake, since they will continue to harden when removed from the oven. Leave to cool completely before decorating.
4. Colour about three-quarters of the royal icing blue and put into a piping bag fitted with a round tip. Pipe an outline around the cookies, and then pipe another outline about 5 mm (¼ in) inside the first outline.
5. Pipe a flame-shaped outline at each end of the cookie and a pointed arc shape in each corner.
6. Add a few drops of water to the remaining blue royal icing and use it to fill a squeezy bottle. Flood the cookies inside the outlines, apart from the corners and the flames (see page 12).
7. Colour about a tablespoon of the royal icing red and thin it with a little water. Use this to fill the flames. Colour about a tablespoon of the royal icing gold and make it thinner. Use this to fill the corners. Leave for a few hours to set.
8. Colour the remaining royal icing gold and fill a piping bag. Pipe over the outlines and add swirls along the border and in the middle of the carpet.
9. When completely dry, paint with edible gold paint.

One day, while in the bazaar, Aladdin met Abanazar, a wicked sorcerer, who persuaded Aladdin to help him find something in return for his own carpet shop.

In a flash, another genie appeared like a wreath of smoke, coming out of the mouth of the lamp.

Magic Lamp Cake Pops

You can bake your own cake to make these pops or use offcuts of cake from other recipes.

MAKES 10–15

- 1 x 10-cm (4-in) round cake (see page 15)
- 300 g (10½ oz) buttercream (see page 19)
- 10–15 cake pop sticks
- 100 g (3½ oz) white chocolate, broken into pieces, or candy melts, melted
- 1 tbsp (20 g) fondant
- Gold food colouring gel
- Gold lustre dust

1. Process the baked cake in a food processor until it forms crumbs.
2. Add some buttercream, a tablespoon at a time, until it starts to come together and forms a dough-like consistency.
3. Take a tablespoon of the mixture and roll it into a ball, then elongate one side to form a long spout and curve it upward.
4. Dip a cake pop stick into the melted white chocolate or candy melts and insert it into the cake pops. Place in the fridge to set.
5. Meanwhile, roll small balls of fondant into long, thin sausages and curve these into an 'S' shape to make the handles. Leave to set.
6. Roll another medium-sized ball of fondant and flatten it for the lid. Attach a small ball of fondant on top of the lid.
7. Attach the handles and the lids to the cake pops using some of the melted white chocolate or candy melts. Place in the fridge to set.
8. Once they have set together, colour the remaining melted white chocolate or candy melts gold. Dip the whole cake pops in the gold-coloured white chocolate or candy melts and place in the fridge to set.
9. When the coating has set, lightly dust with gold lustre dust to make shiny antique-looking lamps.

Gold Piped Macarons

Brushing the piped icing with edible gold paint will turn these macarons into little treasures!

MAKES 15–18

- 70 g (2½ oz) ground almonds
- 100 g (3½ oz) icing sugar
- 2 large egg whites, (approximately 60 ml/2 fl oz)
- ¼ tsp cream of tartar (optional)
- 50 g (1¾ oz) caster sugar
- Assorted food colours (powder or paste)
- 2 tbsp gold royal icing
- Edible gold paint
- 300 g (10½ oz) buttercream or chocolate ganache (see pages 19 and 20)

1. Place the ground almonds and icing sugar in a food processor and process until finely ground. Sift this into another bowl and discard anything that is left in the sieve. Set to one side.
2. Whisk the egg whites until they reach the soft peak stage, then add the cream of tartar (this is optional, but it can help to stabilise the egg). Add the caster sugar, a tablespoon at a time, and continue to whisk until you reach the stiff peak stage.
3. Slowly add the almond/sugar mixture in three batches, folding it in using a spatula in a cut-and-fold action and taking care not to overmix or beat. The mixture should be thick and ribbon-like.
4. Divide the mixture between several small bowls and colour each with your chosen colour. Fill a piping bag fitted with a large round tip and pipe 4-cm (1½-in) discs onto a baking sheet lined with baking parchment.
5. Tap the baking sheet firmly on your work surface a few times and allow to rest for 30–40 minutes until a film has formed. Check this by lightly touching the surface of a macaron – it should not be wet or come off onto your finger. If it is still wet, let it rest for a little longer. Preheat the oven to 150°C (300°F).
6. Once they have rested, bake for 13–15 minutes. The macarons should lift easily from the baking parchment. Allow to cool, then remove from the baking sheet.
7. Pipe patterns on the top of half of the shells using royal icing.
8. Once dry, paint the icing with edible gold paint and leave to dry.
9. Pipe some of your chosen filling (buttercream or chocolate ganache) on the patterned shells, and sandwich together with a plain shell. Set aside to dry for 30 minutes to finish.

Aladdin and his mother asked for food and riches and for a while they were happy.

GINGERBREAD HOUSE (PAGE 68)

FRONT AND BACK PANELS

CUT 2

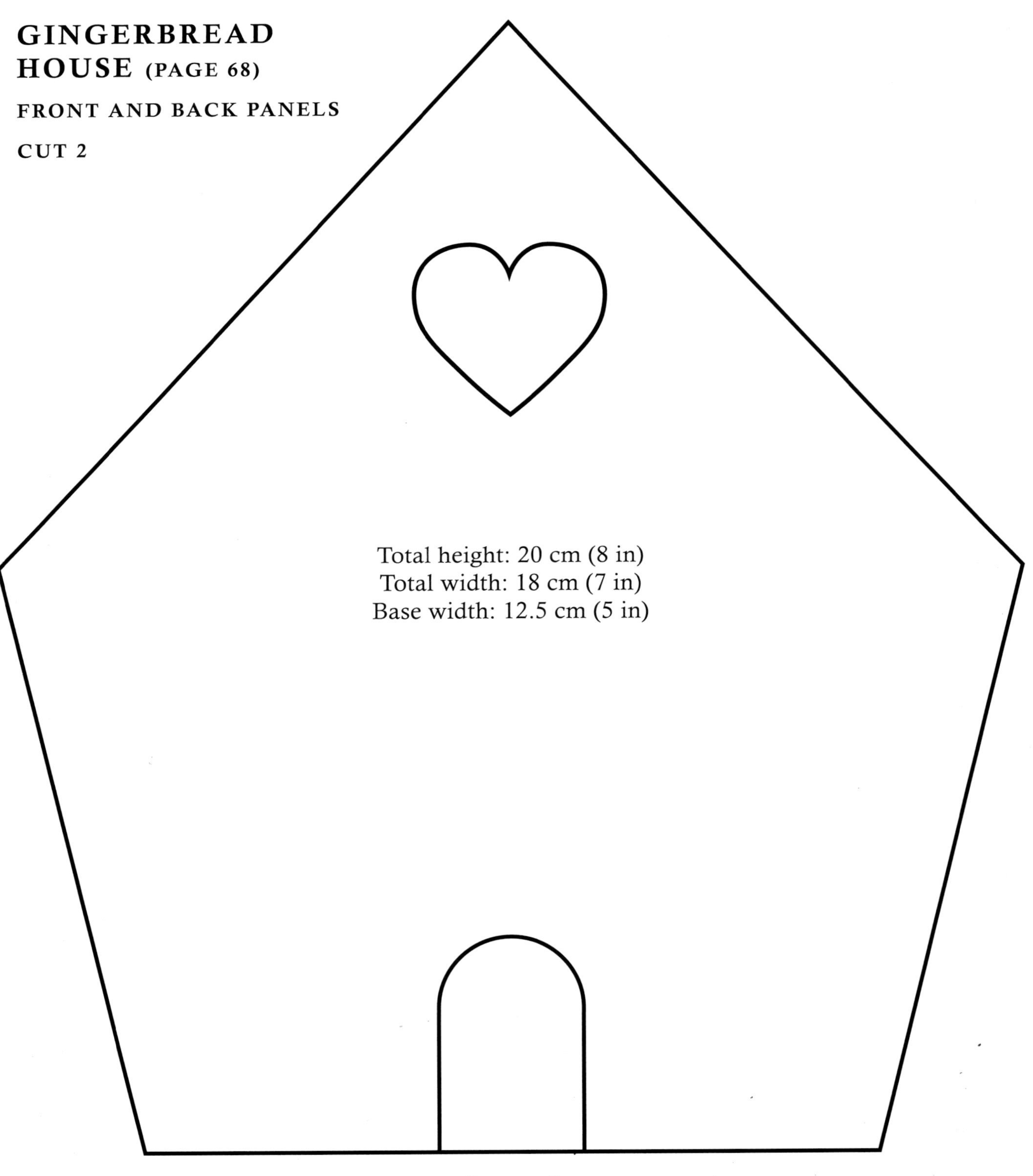

ROOF PANELS

CUT 2

Height: 15 cm (6 in)
Length: 16 cm (6½ in)

GINGERBREAD HOUSE (PAGE 68)

SIDE PANELS

CUT 2

Height: 10.5 cm (4¼ in)
Length: 16 cm (6½ in)

PUMPKIN MINI CAKES (PAGE 40)

COACH DOOR

CUT 1

COACH WHEEL

CUT 4

SLEEPING BEAUTY IN A BED CAKE (PAGE 24)

FRONT BED PANEL

CUT 1

Height: 10 cm (4 in)
Width: 10 cm (4 in)

BACK BED PANEL

CUT 1

Height: 7.5 cm (3 in)
Width: 10 cm (4 in)

BRAMBLE TARTLETS WITH CHOCOLATE THORNS (PAGE 30)

MAGIC CARPET COOKIE (PAGE 176)

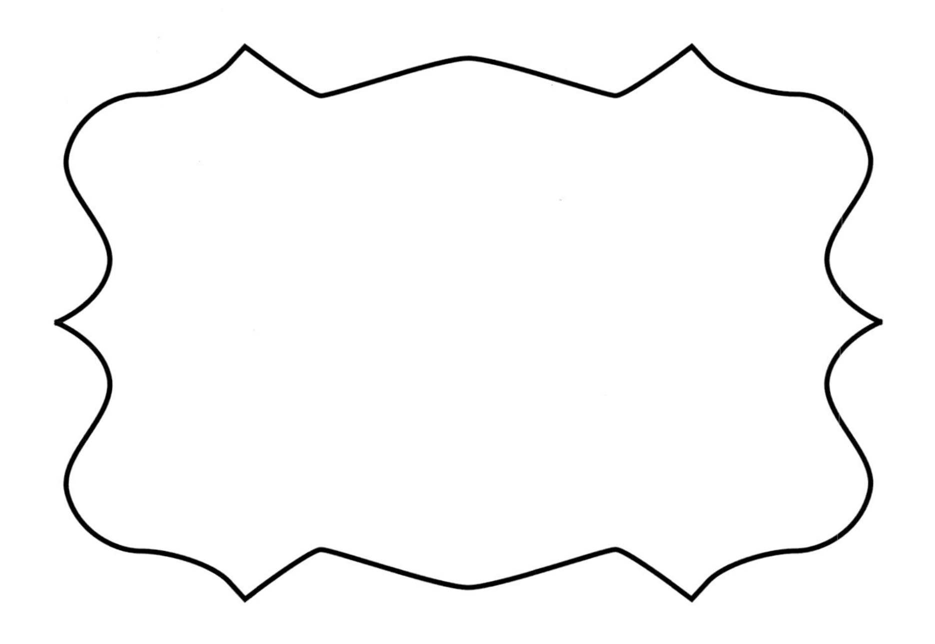

Suppliers

US

CAKE CRAFT SHOPPE
An online store full of baking and cake decorating supplies, including tools and equipment.
3554 Highway 6
Sugar Land, Texas 77478
Tel: 1-281-491-3920
www.cakecraftshoppe.com

GLOBAL SUGAR ART
For fondant, gum paste, colouring and other decorating supplies, including the fondant shoe-making kit for Cinderella's Glass Slipper (see page 42).
1509 Military Turnpike
Plattsburgh, NY 12901
Tel: 1-518-561-3039
Tel: 1-800-420-6088
www.globalsugarart.com

SHOP BAKERS NOOK
Cake decorating, baking and candy-making supplies.
901 West Michigan Avenue
Saline, Michigan 48176
Tel: 1-734-429-1320
www.shopbakersnook.com

WILTON
An international bakeware company that ships worldwide.
Tel: 1-888-373-4588
www.wilton.com

CANADA

GOLDA'S KITCHEN
A retail and online store with a wide range of bakeware and cake decorating supplies, including cake tins, tools and fondant.
2885 Argentia Rd, Unit 6
Mississauga, ON L5N 8G6
Tel: 1-866-465-3299
www.goldaskitchen.com

UK

CAKE CRAFT WORLD
A one-stop shop for all your cake baking and decorating needs.
7 Chatterton Road
Bromley
Kent
BR2 9QW
Tel: 01732 463573
www.cakecraftworld.co.uk

CAKE DECORATING COMPANY
Supplier of cake decorating products, from bakeware to cake lace kits.
Triumph Road
Nottingham, NG7 2GA
Tel: 0115 969 9800
www.thecakedecoratingcompany.co.uk

HOBBYCRAFT
A great source for a range of cake- decorating tools and equipment.
Tel: 0330 026 1400
www.hobbycraft.co.uk

MAKE BAKE
A one-stop shop for sugarcraft supplies and cake decorating equipment.
Tel: 0115 9699848
www.makebake.co.uk

SURBITON SUGARCRAFT
Supplier of cake decorating essentials, from fondant to cake smoothers, cutters and edible decorations.
140 Hook Road
Surbiton, KT6 5BZ
Tel: 020 8391 4664
www.surbitonart.co.uk

Index

This book could not have been written without the encouragement and support of some amazing people who helped me along this journey.

Firstly I'd like to thank my parents and family who have always believed in me and supported me with their love and prayers. They have always encouraged me to nurture my talent and have given me so much valuable advice over the years.

All the team at Quintet for giving me the opportunity to write this book and for supporting me along the way. Michael for his attention to detail, Clare who has done an amazing job of editing my words, and Ella and Jo for their behind-the-scenes work.

The amazing photographers Ian and Simon who are true artists with a camera and have really brought the projects to life.

And finally special thanks go to my husband and chief taste-tester Luqman, without whose total support and patience this book would not have been possible. For enduring the constant mess in the kitchen, the late dinners, and meltdowns at 2am – a huge thank you!